An Ocean Away

by

Betty Worden Mathews

Betty J Mathews

PublishAmerica
Baltimore

First printing

ISBN: 1-4137-0656-8
PUBLISHED BY PUBLISHAMERICA, LLLP
www.publishamerica.com
Baltimore

Printed in the United States of America

This book is dedicated to:
Margot Hoepfner,
who went through it all.

With special thanks to Gary C. Mathews
for the artwork on the front and back cover.

Chapter 1: To the Mountains

Breslau, Germany 1942

Karoline (pronounced Karolina) Mueller moved very slowly. It was dusk, and she was never known for her agility. Twilight in this beautifully landscaped garden back of the Governor's house where she was to meet her papa was making the pretty sixteen-year-old shiver. She was very tired from the constant bombings and their hurry to gather whatever they could to take to the air raid shelters past the huge holes and craters in their streets. Was her papa doing the right thing in asking her mother, sister, auntie, uncle and cousins to go far up into the mountains until the danger of this war was over? She was not afraid to stay in Breslau and didn't want to leave her home or her papa.

Karoline found it hard to miss the dry leaves. She didn't want to make any sounds, and stepping on the dry leaves was sure to make loud crackling sounds. How she wished for the agility of her pretty cousin, Charlotte, who was a year older and always managed to give her the strength she needed in any situation.

Karoline had heard her parents talk about the trouble their city of Breslau was in from the nightly bombings. She knew it was an important industrial city on the Oder River. It was a fortress, *festung,* and because of the ravaging of war, there were only older men left to guard it. Her papa was one of them and felt needed and useful now.

Earlier in the day Alfred Mueller had tried to explain to his wife and young daughters. "Emma, you must take Ereka and Karoline to the mountains until this war is over. The Russian Army is getting too close, and you will not be safe here." Emma knew Alfred was right, but her fear for their future without him made her shudder. Her shaking hands moved up the sides of her smooth, brown, but greying hair, which she kept in a neat bun at the back of her head, and her brown eyes met those of her husband's.

Emma had taken Karoline and Ereka to their chests of drawers in their fourth floor apartment to gather up what clothes they would need for what she felt would be a short stay in the mountains. But her lightheartedness was fading fast. Ereka was a frail six-year-old child who was constantly on the verge of tears. Emma hugged her and helped the girls stuff everything into their small worn bags before they headed down the steep stairs. This south side apartment, such as it was, was the only home they'd ever known. It was a good home and the park was just a block away where the children played

The trip to their grandma and grandpa's home, Emma's parents, Margarete and Heinrich Fendt, was just a 20-mile train ride to the countryside of Breslau. Grandpa Heinrich was a shoemaker by trade, but he loved his job as custodian of the little church nearby. "Run fast, and I will give you candy," he would tease Karoline and Charlotte. He would let them pump the church organ. They visited the church cemetery back of the church following services and take Sunday walks (*spazerein*) then sit on park benches under the shade trees. It was a time to meet friends and go to nearby beer houses where families were always welcome, as was the German custom.

It hadn't been easy for Emma, Ereka and Karoline to get through the rubble without turning their ankles or falling as they moved around the deep craters left by the bombs on their way to the Governor's house. They had tried to hurry, but it had taken longer than they had expected. They dared not miss Alfred as he had made secret arrangements for them to stay there until the train came.

Karoline felt sure her papa had felt much more at ease letting his family go, knowing that Emma's sister, Aunt Eva and Uncle Hermann (who chose not to help guard the city), and her cousin, Charlotte, would go to the mountains with them. Karoline and her cousin had always been best friends.

Her thoughts went back to their first day in school and how their mothers had made their colorfully decorated, cardboard schultutens and filled them with apples, candy and a toy for that most memorable occasion. They had fairly danced along the way as their mothers walked with them to Pestilotste. They took pictures…pictures which were now gone in the bombings, gone forever.

"But, Papa, we would rather stay with you," Karoline had said to him before he had made the decision to send them to the mountains. "We can run down to the bomb shelter ever so fast as soon as we hear the sirens, can't we? Where will we live?" his daughter had asked. At sixteen Karoline was sure she understood more fully than did six-year-old Ereka that they would no longer have a home together.

"Papa, when will you come back for us?" she had persisted as she looked into his worried, somber face. He had said firmly, in his quiet way, that he would come back to say goodbye before they left.

Karoline thought about her parents and how different they were from one another. Though she was inclined to be more like her papa, she wanted so to be lighthearted and fun-loving like her *mutti*. Hitler's army had rejected Alfred, who was blind in one eye from an arrow that had gone astray during what had begun as an exciting childhood game of "Indians and Trappers." Karoline knew her papa was not a strong, brave man, but also that he needed to feel better about himself. Her mind spun with these thoughts and of the many wonderful afternoons she had spent with him ice skating on those cold, crisp winter days of winter and then swimming on the same lake in the heat of summer.

When Alfred and Emma married, the family felt it was definitely not a marriage "made in Heaven" as his family was catholic and hers protestant, but the two surprised all who were concerned with their love and happiness.

When he lost his job, his parents took him, Emma, and Karoline in and sent him to bakery school as they felt that at least he would always be able to feed his family. Daily, Alfred rode his bike to the factory and soon became a master of his trade. His new job as a baker enabled them to find their apartment on the fourth floor in south Bresslau, not far from the park.

But Emma shuddered when she thought back to just before Ereka was born. She knew she should have been happy to be expecting a new life to join their family. Her thoughts of Hitler's new laws about sterilizing people "unfit for reproducing" hadn't applied to her. Birth control for Aryans, those with four German grandparents, was not allowed, and pregnancies could *not* be terminated without a very good reason. Hitler wanted an *Aryan* race...only the best! But times were so unsettling Emma worried about the new life she would bring into this world.

Emma thought about the two years of Nazi rule that had brought about some new, puzzling laws. She was nervous. She sat on the couch, picking at the green and yellow hand-embroidered flowers on the pillow cover. Her brown hair was smoothed and brought back into a thick braid then wound in a tight circle at the nape of her neck. After some silence, she moved closer to her sister.

"Emma, what is it?" Eva whispered. Emma didn't answer right away. She looked around the room, then rose and walked to the window. Cautiously, she peered under the fringed window shade before turning to her sister.

"Eva, the Nazis will not allow us to shop in any Jewish store any more! We are to boycott them all!" she said in a hoarse, fearful voice. "Under the Ministry of Propaganda, Joseph Goebbels, even our daughters' books seem to condemn the Jews. His posters and handbills blame the Jews for everything! There is a movie called Jud Suss (The Jew Suss), Goebbels' inspiration, which is very popular in Berlin and across Germany, which makes people think killing Jews would be all right!

"Both the Howitz children and their parents must wear the yellow star of David where it can be seen. We cannot even invite Jews to our suppers or meetings. We must not SPEAK to those Jewish who have been our dear friends! This is the law of the party...and we must obey!"

Eva's hands went to her face. She paused for what seemed an eternity before answering her sister.

"Emma, what are we to do? Ilse and I sew together every Wednesday, and she teaches me French seams." The room was still except for the loud ticking of the Black Forest cuckoo clock on the wall.

"And our girls cannot play with Joel and little Harriett any more? How can we explain to them, or keep them apart?" Eva wailed. She got up and walked across the room to the couch, trembling.

"We will have to walk far to buy our food now," she whispered, pausing. "Harriett and Abe's store is the only one close by."

"Eva, someone, *anyone,* can report us if we don't obey these orders of the Fuhrer," Emma told her sister firmly.

"There are stories all around us about the Gestapo taking away those who have not listened; even the teacher, Mrs. Bauer, who spoke against some of these laws was taken away from her home! Some say she is in prison! We cannot even take this problem to our church, Eva. Their state aid has been cut off. Church schools are being closed! The Catholic Women's Organization is trying to keep Nazi doctrine out of their schools, because any issue seems to end up with political overtones. When church officials negotiate with the Nazis, it almost always ends with the Nazis winning and the church compromising. Now the Nazi National Socialist Party rules!"

"Emma, how do we love *and* hate??" We *must* look the other way. What can just families like ours do against such strict law enforcement? Even if we started petitions or tried to object, we might be sent to prison, too. Then what would happen to our girls?"

The sisters sat in silence. The small cuckoo clock that hung above the overstuffed couch, broke the silence as it struck three and the little bird appeared to dip its beak up and down.

"Eva, do you remember Helga Graff? She has been in prison for many months. Hew *own* cousin reported her because Helga let her children play with Jewish younsters. The Fuhrer calls Jews pigs! Helga was very active in school social functions, but she spoke up against the new laws."

"How could they do that to such a good person?" Eva asked her sister in a fearful whisper.

Just then, the back door slammed shut, and both sisters jumped nervously when Karoline and Charlotte ran into the room crying, yelling. "Mutti, Aunt Eva, we can't find Joel! He doesn't live at the store any more! We stopped to ask Joel and Harriett to play, and no one lives there!" squealcd Karoline and Charlotte in barely understandable voices.

"We looked everywhere for them!" added the girls as they choked and sobbed out their story. Neither Emma nor Eva could speak. Had the Howitzes already been taken away?

With great effort Emma said, "Go now, girls, wash your hands, and we will give you cookies before we work some more on your schultutes." Emma tried hard to be the laughing mutti she knew her daughter expected her to be, but when their daughters left the room, the mothers held one another in a tearful embrace.

In the days that followed, Ilse Bauer, a neighbor, pretended to be tending her flowers at the backyard fence, but in a low voice she called to Emma.

"Emma, last night my Heinrich saw two big, stern-looking ladies go to the Howitz's door. They were dressed in dark, long coats and wore heavy shoes. Their hair was funny, he said, and looked like it was glued to their heads!" Then Ilse lowered her voice even more, looked around cautiously, and added, "They had black bags and banged really hard on the Howitz's door. My Heinrich saw the door open, and then he saw those ladies go in. He waited a long time…until he got too cold…and didn't see them come out. You know what, Emma? Last week my cousins, the Luders, saw the same thing happen to two Jewish families in their neighborhood!"

Neighbors began to whisper about Jewish friends going to ghettos and work camps where, once there, one of their own is picked to govern his people.

Karoline shivered with fright as she waited for her father's shadowy form to appear through the swaying branches. "Papa, here I am, over here," she whispered as loudly as she dared. He grasped his daughter in his arms and whispered quietly, "Now you must go right back and tell your *mutti* and your little sister to come. I will do my best to guard our city and keep our home safe so we can come back to it," he told his daughter. They hugged one another and said not another word until Alfred said, "Goodbye for now, my daughter!" Slowly, he turned and walked toward the dark street. Hot tears slid down Karoline's cheeks as she stumbled through the garden then turned to catch a last glimpse of him. When would she see him again? When would they ever have a real home again? That was the last time Karoline ever saw her beloved papa.

Chapter 2: The War Is Over

Karoline shuddered in the crisp night air as she walked back slowly to her mutti and little sister. Ereka seemed unable to stop her crying. Maybe when they met her auntie, uncle, and her cousin, Charlotte, things would be different. They would find a place to sit and wait for the train and Mutti could hold her. "Here's a bench!" Karoline pointed excitedly, for she had no idea how long a wait they would have.

It was early morning when the whistle pierced the cold, crisp air, and it sent chills through every bone in Karoline's body. She saw the white, puffy steam belching in spurts in its efforts to reach the rolling, white clouds racing across the blue sky. The engine chugged and jerked to a screeching halt as it let lose its gasping steam.

Loaded with possessions, the immigrants moved slowly along the platform with hopes of getting on the train, whether there were seats or not. Emma guided her young ones up the black, metal steps and into the first car where many of the passengers were already standing. The air was thick with body odors, the smell of old leather suitcases and even mothballs. It was so stuffy it was hard to breath where the girls were standing, but Karoline felt relief when she saw her mutti sit down with Ereka.

"At least we can put our bags near Mutti," she whispered to Charlotte, "and we can hold onto this seat." Every so often, they would look through the foggy windows and catch a glimpse of the snow-covered, glistening mountains above dense stands of dark, green pines as the train chugged higher and higher into the beautiful, snow-covered mountains. Neither of the girls had ever seen such scenery and whispered excitedly to one another as they rubbed circles of steam on the shrouded windows for a clearer view.

"Look, Charlotte, the mountains reach right up to Heaven!" Karoline whispered excitedly to her cousin. It was probably the first smile she'd managed since they'd left their home in Breslau after such a sad goodbye to her papa. Even looking through the dingy windows made the two teenagers squint from the bright sunshine, but this would be a train trip they would never forget.

When they reached the tiny, remote, country town of Opeln in the Glazer Gaberge Range, all the travelers got out at the marketplace to await the mayor's arrival. The girls were nervous. Charlotte, at 17, had always felt some responsibility toward Karoline, who was a year younger. They'd been friends and school chums since their early years. But Karoline was so terribly shy and seemed to need the support of her more outgoing cousin. When the mayor arrived, he and the townspeople gathered around to talk about what they could do with all their fellow countrymen, these homeless imigrants.

"You will all be placed in homes somewhere around here," the mayor announced in his most positive voice. "You will be sent up into a little village." Now the girls were even more fearful of their stay. His words soon reached the farmers who came to the marketplace with their snorting, shiny horses and colorful sleighs to pick up the weary travelers. The girls had heard or read about sleighbells, but now they were actually hearing them as the prancing horses jostled their heads back and forth. In her fear of this unknown happening in her young life, Karoline looked around for Emma and Ereka. At 16, she had never been without a home.

Karoline's feelings of being alone, even though Charlotte was with her, almost made her sick as she thought back to the worst time of her life when she was six years old.

As if it was yesterday, she remembered sitting on her loving vater's lap up in their fourth floor apartment in Breslau in those quiet, peaceful years. Mutti called, in her lilting, sing-song voice, "Bath time, Karoline!" It was once-a-week bath time, and Emma had her daughter's water ready in the old metal tub in the cozy, warm kitchen on the floor next to the stove. They had to sign up a week ahead to wash clothes in the apartment, but Friday night was always bath night and signing wasn't necessary.

Then came Mutti's voice again in that singing way Karoline loved. She disliked leaving her vater's lap and wanted to object, but Alfred gave her a loving shove, and she sauntered, feeling ever so tired, toward the kitchen.

Pulling off her daughter's dress and the wool stockings, held up by the hated leibchen, Emma thought Karoline felt warmer than usual. Fearfully, she looked at the child's small hands. There they were, the dreaded red spots and blisters. She looked into Karoline's hazel, glazed eyes and at the parched, red lips.

"Alfred! Come look at Karoline!" she called with an urgency in her voice that her husband recognized instantly. With one look at his little girl's red-spotted, warm body, he knew the worst. The frightening epidemic of scarlet fever had made its ugly appearance into their home!

Quarantine! The Muellers were required to take their six-year-old daughter to the hospital and leave her there, without them, alone, for six weeks! It was for the sake of the baby, the doctor had told them, that child whose arrival had caused Karoline such pain these past months. How she hated that baby.

For six lonely weeks Karoline lay very ill on the hard, white hospital bed. The terrible loneliness she felt so young had never left her. She cried so often that the nurse said, "Karoline, please try to think only of your best memories, always." Today, so many years later, she *still* attempted to heed that nurse's advice. "Help me," she whispered into her small, gloved hands to a Being she new would listen.

There wasn't room enough in one home for her aunt, uncle and all of them, so she and Charlotte were told they would stay in the mayor's home. "Your family will not be far away from you," the mayor said, "and they will be taken by wagons to homes nearby."

The sun shown on the white snow amidst the tall pines, and the farmer put the girls in the rear seat of the sleigh under warm blankets as the lively team pranced gracefully, in their squeaking, leather harnesses, anxiously awaiting their signal to swish forward.

The girls threw their heads back and laughed excitedly, (how long had it been?) as if they hadn't a care in the world as they listened to the music of the jingling, silver bells around the animal's lurching necks! It was a world of wonder and beauty that two teenagers of a war-torn country would never forget, a wonderland they had never seen! They listened to the sounds of the sleigh scrunching and swishing its way up and down narrow, snow-covered trails as the farmer urged his team with gentle commands. The sounds of "pppfff, pppfff" from the horses nostrils as they blew their visible breaths with each jerk of their necks in the crisp, cold mountain air would stay with Karoline and Charlotte forever! What did they care about an advancing Russian army?

Once settled in the mayor's home, the cousins walked almost daily through the beautiful rolling countryside to visit their families. They found Emma and Ereka to be the happiest they could remember seeing them. Of course the new visitors were expected to do their share. They could care for tiny Hans, cook and clean. The best part was that there was food enough for all. Another great feeling for all of them was that the war was almost over. They heard no bombs, planes and no longer had to hide in cellars. Spring was coming, and the girls had never felt this safe.

One evening a whole caravan of probably 100 Russian soldiers made camp in their village. The officer asked where the mayor's home was. "My men will stay in your barn," he said, "and my associate and I will stay in your home," he told the mayor.

Because the girls were staying in the mayor's home, they talked over their problem. Charlotte, usually the leader, said, "Karoline we must look our worst. We should put scarves over our heads, bend over to look older and wear our oldest clothes." They both agreed, but still felt vulnerable, so along with other ladies, they sneaked to the attic and pushed furniture in front of the bedroom door. They were lying all over the floor and on the bed. Suddenly, when it seemed all was quiet, there was a knock ar their door. Silence. Then came a louder knock, soon followed by another.

"We want to see you!" came a male voice. The women and girls could hear others talking. They were almost afraid to breath. One of the ladies tried to sound very old and said, "Go away! I am old and very sick!" No one moved. They could feel their hearts pounding in their throats. Minutes of silence followed. They dared not move. Then came the sounds of heavy footsteps going down the stairs. Though everyone seemed to breath easier, they still said nothing. No sounds came from their attic room. What if one of the men stayed behind? This was the foremost thought in their minds.

It seemed hours, but was probably only ten minutes later when they rose from their blankets and tiptoed to the window of the third-floor room. They peered cautiously from behind the curtains. It was just twilight. On the streets below they could see soldiers everywhere milling around.

It was then that Karoline thought of the night her mutti had sat her down and told her what to do if something like this ever happened to her. "Karoline, if you are ever accosted and someone really wants to hurt you, you must let them do exactly what they want to do...no matter how frightened you are. If you don't, they will kill you. Do you understand? Do not ever forget that!" Emma stressed this to her again. Karoline always did exactly as her parents asked her to and seldom answered back. "I will try to do as you say, Mutti."

Suddenly, the night air was rent with horrendous screams! Doors slammed. Mothers yelled for help with their daughters. Girls were being dragged out of their houses. Terrible, blood-curdling screams and cries of "No...PLEASE DON'T!" reached the ears of those in the mayor's upstairs attic room.

Karoline and Charolotte looked at each other, their hands to their mouths. Raucous male laughter filled the evening air. Sounds of heavy feet running up the road went on for a very long time. Those in the stuffy, seemingly secure, small attic room didn't dare move. It was then the girls realized they had barely escaped a similar fate! They shivered as they lay next to each other. "Please God, don't let them return," Karoline whispered.

When the fitful, long night ended and dawn broke, the lady two doors down the road knocked on the kitchen door below them. They heard her enter the mayor's home, and the mayor's wife asked her to sit down. The girls tiptoed down the stairs as far as they dared so they could see the woman. She was still shaking and could barely talk from her terrifying experiences of the night.

"My husband and I took our daughter into the barn and hid her underneath us," she said quietly. "We pulled straw all around us." Her voice quivered as she told her story. "It was terrible. We were so frightened. We were so afraid they would come in and find us. But they didn't!"

The sun was coming up, and its early morning rays filtered through the tall pine's graceful branches as the soldiers congregated near the clear, rippling waters of the small stream that moseyed through the village. Only yesterday, it had been a quiet, safe and lovely village. *How could they ever leave this room?* they wondered.

Chapter 3: Walking to Breslau

Karoline and Charlotte continued to stay in the little attic room of the mayor's house. How could they be sure the Russian soldiers were gone? Their vigilance in looking out the curtained window every half hour to check the area by the little stream made them feel safer. They took turns. As they lay under the covers, Karoline said softly to her cousin, "I don't think we did the right thing the other day when we went to the barn and that German soldier whispered for us to us to come over to him. But how could we not go to him when he was so hungry and alone?"

When the soldier said "This way…over here…pitte!" the girls had moved closer to investigate. He was covered with hay and was near the stall. "I will give you some beer," he called anxiously, still barely above a whisper. "C'mon you should drink with me!" he said, laughing at their surprised look. "I have left my unit, and I am very hungry. Could you bring me something to eat?"

The girls knew they were taking a big chance when they told the lonely, hungry soldier they would try to come back to the barn after supper that night. But they knew he was hungry. And he *was* German.

As soon as they finished washing the supper dishes, they filled their pockets with leftover bread and cheese. As soon as the mayor's wife went out of the kitchen, they left for their walk.

They were both giddy with excitement and kept looking all around as they made their way back to the barn. It was easy to find him. And he was so happy to see them and so thankful for the food it made them feel good they could help a fellow countryman. He wolfed everything down, then grabbed the startled girls and said, "I kiss you for this!" He was very strong, but they weren't really frightened when they accepted his kisses with giggles. "Danka! Danka!!" he kept repeating as he let go of them. They were more afraid of being discovered than they were of him!

"Come, Charlotte, we must hurry back or we will be missed," Karoline said to her pretty, blonde cousin as she pulled hard to drag her away from their soldier.

"Goodbye," Charlotte called, "we will see you after the war. All right?"

Their reminiscing had only just begun. It was all there was to do, and they loved some of the memories of their days in Breslau before the bombings tore their city apart.

"Remember what fun we had in our park, Charlotte? Mutti cleaned her carpet on the *klopfpfstange*, and the dust flew below the chestnut trees. It was spring, and the sun splashed warm rays through the shade-tree limbs as Friedrich, Joel, Harriett you and I got down on our knees to play marbles?

"Then remember that one day when everything in our lives changed? A raucous, earsplitting roar of something overhead broke the quiet of our afternoon. Everyone looked up and then at each other. We all stopped playing. We looked at each other wide-eyed!

'What is it? What is it?' we yelled. First one of us then an other got up and started running for home. I remember brushing the dirt from my knees and running as fast as I could. 'Mutti! Mutti!!' I yelled as I stumbled and fell. I sobbed until I reached the top of our four flights of stairs and fell into my mutti's arms. Tears splashed down my red cheeks as I sobbed and mutti hugged and rocked me.

"My mutti said, 'You have just heard the motor of an airplane, Karoline,' and then in an uneasy voice she added, 'It may not be the last of such loud sounds you'll hear.'

"She was really right, wasn't she Charlotte?"

It was Charlotte's turn to look out the window, and though she didn't know if he was a Russian soldier, she did see a man she hadn't seen before, so they snuggled further under the blanket as they talked about their past.

"Mostly I remember, Charlotte, when the Fuhrer said all of us had to go into Hitler Youth when we were ten, and you said you weren't going to go to the Bund Deutsche Madchen for the League of German girls!

My mutti said it was the law and you would have to obey it, and I was so afraid to go without you. They wanted me to be a leader, but I knew I couldn't do that, as I was too shy. Mutti made me go without you. In three days they came after you!! I wasn't nearly as afraid to go those three days after school from four to five o'clock because you were with me." Charlotte pushed her blonde hair out of her eyes and smiled at her cousin who made her feel so important. "Remember how we chanted, 'Be faithful, be pure, be German!' and camped and marched, sang and did athletics at meetings and wore our navy skirts and white blouses?"

Hitler held a definite grip on his members of Hit!er Youth. According to the Time Life Books series he wrote, "A man of small intellectual attainment, but physically healthy, is more valuable to the national community than an educated weakling." Hitler Youth emphasized physical training through hikes, muscle building and combat games that would focus on the group rather than the individual. The groups had weekly meetings of interest to all with singing, field days and teams for competition. Hitler wanted strong youth who would one day fight for Germany and sports readily emphasized were those of potential military application. Sailing aboard naval vessels, racing the countryside on motorcycles, enjoying flights in bombers and fighters gave way to training for the navy, motorized storm troopers and glider action.

But another law Hitler began enforcing terrified Karoline. He said that all girls at age 14 had to do "household" for a year, which meant each girl went to another family to learn to do housework, care for children and learn to cook. Karoline's parents studied the papers and looked carefully for a home they thought sounded right for her. Girls could go daily and return to their parents' homes at night, or live with the family training them and go home one weekend a month. They would be "mother's helpers."

Karoline's parents had no car, and the home they chose for their daughter (because they felt she would have good food) was ten miles across Breslau from them. She was allowed to call home periodically, and could take a bus home on her one weekend a month. But her homesickness prevailed for two months, and when she called home, she began to cry. Her mother insisted she stay, so Karoline learned from the landscape architect and his wife, Frau and Herr Frommel. Frau Frommel took flowers to the hospital and her husband cared for his beautiful yard and productive greenhouse. The couple had two children and a goat, and Herr Frommel raised exotic or fancy flowers. Karoline slept in the children's room with them, cared for the two young ones and also took care of the goat. It wasn't funny for the household the night the goat got loose and began eating the architect's prized plants. He was so furious he threw dishes at his wife, and they argued loudly!

Germany had been suffering from drastic unemployment in 1933. Misery and economic chaos had been a way of life for the last decade and a half under Marxism. The German people desperately needed a leader who could stop the Communists. Hadn't their new Chancellor, Adolph Hitler, promised to build the autobahn? Hadn't he said there would be jobs for all, and milk and butter for the children? He loved his children and would not let them starve: and he would see to it that they would have gatherings for marching, singing, laughing, camping and athletics they would enjoy.

Their industrial port city of Breslau of about 650,000 was a rail junction 180 miles east, southeast of Berlin along the 563-mile-long Oder River. It was a major manufacturing center for machinery. The historic city was known for its Gothic Churches, a 13th century cathedral and a 14th and 15th century town hall.

Emma and Alfred's friends had recently attended a party rally and told Emma what excitement there had been. She related it all to Alfred. He just looked at his frau. He said nothing.

"Alfred, isn't our workers trade union much larger than the Nazi Party membership? So we don't have to worry too much if we disagree with the new laws, do we?"

He thought awhile before he answered. "No, maybe not, Emma, but let us not get interested in joining the party, even if we are asked.

There are some very strong measures I don't agree with. I did not like hearing about the victory parade in Hamburg when the brown shirts sang battle songs like, "The Republic Is Shit!" Worse yet, Emma, was when they said, "Today we rule Germany, tomorrow the world!"

Emma and Eva read in the newspapers where Gertrude Scholtz-Klink was Hitler's Reichsfrauenfuhrerun, or thought she was his "right hand lady," and could make a difference in his ideas, and tried to lead millions of German ladies with her ideas. The sisters felt great resentment to Scholtz-Klink's ideas, including telling them how many children they should have! "Last week she told us what to cook and now this week she tells us what to wear!" exclaimed an exasperated Emma who added, "Another thing, that Klink woman has some nerve to tell us how to act if one of our loved ones is killed! We couldn't laugh and shrug it off if one of our men is killed, like that twitty mother who let Hitler touch her shoulder with his compassion. She looked like she worshiped him!" Eva added, "Hitler bought our library and said he was going to buy all of the school libraries if they were Jewish, or not German, and that's not all; those ladies that work for the city are turning in all the names of those little ones who can't quite think right, and if there's a mother who isn't right in the head and she's pregnant, they will take her baby," Eva sniffed. "I don't know, Emma; everything is so different now. What will it be next?"

The sisters read about the Protestant Women's leader Agnes Von Grone who was supposed to bring their organizations in line and created an agency for them called Frauenwerk, or Women's Bureau. She was the Reichsfrauenfuhrerin of the two-and-a-half million Protestant women in January, 1934...but the Nazis eventually won out.

German business women also reported suspicious strangers in neighborhoods, while haus fraus kept old traditions alive, gave charity to the poor, sewed for the brown shirts, cared for the SA men and cooked for rallies. All women under 25 were in service if not in war work.

Karoline and Charlotte had been watching the streets of the little village for hours and had seen nothing or none to cause them any trouble, so they decided to go down to talk to the mayor's wife and tell her of their wish to walk to see the rest of the family. The kindly mayor's wife told them the war was now over and that they'd not have to fear more bombings. Their only fear now was the straggling soldiers of the Russian army.

Suddenly a new problem faced these now homeless people. Where would they go? And how would they get there? They had no horses, no bicycles no money to buy anything to help them. There were no stores in which they could buy anything, even if they did have the money! They had to get back to Breslau some way to see if there was anything left of their home and to find out if Alfred was still there.

Chapter 4: Woods

Uncle Herman told the group, "We will all stay together. Russian soldiers are roving the countryside, but if we stay together, we should be safe. It is settled," he added in his German firmness. "This would be a very long walk of at least sixty miles," someone of the group said.

They had few belongings but had the food their wonderful host people had given them to carry on their cart. They pulled their cart, or in some cases, a small wagon, down the quiet, country road. It was not paved but splattered with bunches of gravel thrown along the sides by trucks and army equipment. Some of the dry, hard soil was exposed where wheels often traveled, but the beauty and curves of the old, former lane remained. The rays of the sun penetrated the graceful branches of evergreens, framing the road formed short, dark shadows rather than bright, yellow streaks of different widths. Charlotte and Karoline, bored with walking, played a competitive game to see who could jump the widest sun patches. Finally they were giggly, happy teenagers.

Thick, green bushes also lined the roadsides, concealing the dense forest beyond. They encountered countless curves which made it seem as hard to pull the wagon downhill as it did up. The route was narrow, and the afternoon shadows grew deeper. Some of the twenty or more travelers were growing weary and began talking about places to stay for the night.

"We could stay in the woods under big trees," Emma suggested. But Aunt Eva and Uncle Hermann thought they should have something over their heads. It wasn't long before the road leveled out and Uncle Herman pointed ahead.

"Let's look at that old barn up on our right. It looks like a safe place, and it isn't so damaged!" There wasn't a *nein* to be heard.

"We could stop early and eat; then there would be enough daylight so we could find a place to sleep," someone said. Instinctively, everyone in the group knew the importance of rationing their food supply, as they had no idea when they would get more. There were no stores. Even if there were stores, they had no money.

The straggling groups stumbled across the unkept stubble-covered fields. Some went to look at the weathered, vine-smothered house, as Karoline, Charlotte, Emma and Ereka talked about the family who must surely have enjoyed living in this beautiful, country setting. They started for the barn.

The Hellwigs and Muellers kept together as they entered the barn through a dangling, weatherbeaten door. It hung from rusty, creaking hinges. As they stepped inside, unsuspecting birds screamed and flew wildly through the rafters, sending clouds of dust through rays of late afternoon sunlight that filtered through the wide set barn siding.

"Mutti! MUTTI!! What is it?" Karoline and Charlotte shrieked as Karoline grabbed for her mother. "It's all right, girls. We have just frightened the birds who have been living in this barn for a long time with no one to disturb them," consoled a nervous Emma.

With new feelings of security, the girls took off through the dusty straw to find the perfect place to spend the night. The spot they chose had once been part of the pig's pen, Emma reminded them; but they were in such good moods they threw themselves into their "beds," saying gleefully, "We don't care! And we have a roof over our heads!"

"Look, Charlotte, we can put our blanket right here, and use some of the straw to cover up with," shouted Karoline excitedly to her cousin. Several others of the group were also in the barn, so when darkness fell, the weary young travelers felt safe. They had no trouble falling asleep.

Birds were chirping when the sun pierced the wide cracks in the shrunken barn siding the next morning, and the girls took one look at each other and began laughing hysterically! "Look at you, Charlotte," cried Karoline, "you're covered with flies!"

"So are you!" retorted the other.

With loud laughter, they danced up and down as they slapped at the hundreds of sticky, lethargic insects and woke all the others who stumbled sleepily over to investigate the commotion.

Before leaving the old barn and the weather-beaten, vine-covered house, everyone went out into the field to hunt for potatoes. They felt sure their hunt would be successful, even if the vines had almost disappeared, as potatoes had been the key field crop of Germany since the 1700s.

As they found evidence of a vine, they tried digging, but without a shovel, it wasn't easy. If they couldn't find sticks, they used their hands. Sticks usually broke as they penetrated the hardened ground. When a potato was found, they quickly stashed it into their clothes and the wagons. They knew their food was sure to run out and the potatoes could even save their lives.

Ereka showed her mutti the dirt and grime on her hands, and Emma had them all rub their hands on the dew-covered, tall grasses to get rid of some of the dirt. They could hear Aunt Eva yelling for them to catch up with them and tell them to never stay far behind.

The beautiful, tree-lined road stretched before them; and after walking about an hour, the girls decided to make a relief stop. Charlotte yelled to their mothers, who were a few hundred yards ahead, that she and Karoline were going into the bushes and would soon catch up. "All right, but hurry!" warned their mothers.

Giggling and chatting, they started plodding through the thick vines and brush. Cobwebs glistened in the morning light and kept the girls busy dodging the spiders. It was hard to keep from tripping over the tangled roots. Charlotte, always the more aggressive, said, "I'm going back farther." Several minutes lapsed. She found what she thought was the best place for her utmost comfort. She didn't want to tear her only good dress, so carefully pulled it up around her waist and anchored it in her panties. Branches snapped just behind her. Startled, she looked up to see three Russian soldiers crashing through the bushes toward her. She screamed and started to run as fast as she could. Emma and Eva were too far ahead to hear her cries for help. Karoline, many feet back, clasped her hands over her mouth and stood still, SO frightened she couldn't move.

She could hear her cousin running deeper into the woods. Screaming. Charlotte tried to hurdle the twisted vines. Run! RUN!! She kept telling herself. She could hear the laughing, gruff-sounding soldiers getting closer. She knew they could see her now.

Karoline could hear the soldiers as they caught up with her frantic cousin. She stopped moving and kept her small, shaking hands over her mouth. As they caught up with the shaking girl, Charlotte was screaming and yelling for them to leave her alone. Her cries for help made Karoline shake and cry in fear. Never in her whole life had she felt so helpless. Even the bombings and running to the air raid shelters hadn't affected her like this!

Karoline heard them throw Charlotte onto the ground. The pretty, blonde, long-legged girl kicked and screamed as hard as she could. Her blonde braids twisted across her pretty face, and her eyes were red and tear-filled as she yelled, "Don't touch me! Stop, you're dirty!! I HATE YOU!!" She fought frantically. Branches were breaking as the men laughed and mocked their prey. The three men grabbed both her arms and her long, kicking legs as they ripped off all her clothes. With all the strength she had left, she kicked one between his legs. He doubled over. In his new fury, he wielded a mighty blow to the seventeen-year-old's head, and Karoline heard the sickening thud. The screaming stopped. She lay before them completely immobile. Blood oozzed down the side of her head and into her blond braid.

I've got to run away from here, Karoline cried as tears streamed down her face. *I've got to hide*, she told herself as she tried to run through the thick brush. Frantically, she looked for a downed log behind which to hide. How she wished she could run as fast as her cousin could. *God...I pray you to help me...PLEASE!*

Though she was running for her life, she tripped. She fell hard. An old rotten log was close by, and she crawled behind it, shaking so hard the vines were moving. Loud cursing reached her ears. She was afraid to move. I have to hold my breath.

Suddenly, all the noise stopped. She heard the heavy, thudding footsteps. They were coming her way. Closer, now.

"We can find her. Look at these bushes. She went this way," she was sure they were saying. She could hear them chuckling. *If I run, maybe I can make it back to the road. I have to try. They will find me here,* she told herself as she got up to leave her hiding place.

Her mutti had always told her if she was captured NOT to fight, just let them have what they wanted or they will kill you. "Can you remember that, Karoline?!!" Emma had asked firmly. Karoline had said yes. Of course the pretty, curly-haired brunette never thought she would be in such a position. It had been after the girls in the little village near the mayor's house had been so brutally raped that her mutti pulled her aside and warned her in such a way.

The more Karoline thought about this, the harder she ran. Their hideous laughing was coming closer. Heavy footsteps were crashing through the brush right behind her. The thick vines were slowing her down, and her shaking was slowing her progress. She was getting weak. Her lungs ached.

"This way!" shouted one. "Yes, YES!!!" shouted another. It wasn't hard to guess what they were saying. Sobbing and parting the twisted vines made her gasp for air. They soon caught up with the frantic sixteen-year-old.

"Ah HAH!" said the one who grabbed her skirt. He pulled it so hard it ripped. It slid to her ankles, and her feet got caught in it. She fell into the bushes with the skirt twisted around her legs. Trapped. The other two men grabbed her arms. "No! NO!! she cried as she sobbed as they pulled her blouse apart. They held her arms tightly and looked with great eagerness at their pretty, young prize.

Down on their knees, they began murmuring soft, sweet German words to her as they pulled her blouse off and began to fondle her small, firm breasts. Their hands were rough. Their panting so close to her face only made their smelly breaths more distasteful. The one closest to her had yellow teeth which protruded, and they all laughed as she begged them to let go of her. She wanted to throw up. "God, please help me, or I'll die!" she begged.

They tore her undergarments off as they laughed and talked to each other in Russian. She could see the blood on their pants...Charlotte's!

Her sobs were wracking her slim body as they studied her with obvious admiration. "Please let me live! Don't hurt me!" she begged hysterically. Her strength to fight was almost gone.

They began taking their dirty, blood-stained pants down. They held her arms. Her heart was pounding so that she thought it might burst. In halting German, one of them said, "C'mon my pretty one…you will like it if you don't fight us! Then we won't hurt you!" he grinned through his dirty mustache and dark whiskers.

"Now…just lie quietly in this nice, soft moss…QUIETLY!" he added firmly. His blazing dark eyes flashed in eagerness at her naked body as he adjusted her shaking form on the bed of moss.

"Please…PLEASE don't!" she begged as she threw her head from side to side.

"Come. Be quiet, my pretty!" he said as he ran his hands down her nude, shaking body.

What she saw made her close her tear-filled eyes. Shivering violently she tried to stop sobbing.

"Mutti…mutti!" she whispered as she stopped fighting the inevitable.

One on each side of her suckled her breasts as the other threw himself on top of her. She shrieked in pain. Warm blood began oozing down her thighs. Each took his turn.

When it was over, she covered her face as they pulled their clothes on. She couldn't look. Then they started running…deeper into the forest.

Karoline lay very still. She couldn't move. She was numb all over. Finally, as she opened her eyes and looked around her, the sun gleamed through the bushes and shown on her own blood as it trickled further into the moss. Never had she felt so dirty. "Charlotte, Charlotte, I'm coming," she called as she struggled painfully to get up to go to her cousin.

Birds of the forest were chirping and singing. How could they? She found her ripped clothes and tried to put them on. Her hands were trembling. It was easy to follow the paths of those savage men. When she reached the pretty blonde cousin whom she loved so dearly, Charlotte was not moving.

Karoline gasped and threw herself down next to her. She tried to cover and warm the cold, badly bruised girl. "Charlotte…CHARLOTTE, please talk to me," she sobbed. The thick, long braids were matted with blood and laying across her face. Then she saw it. A deep, dark, blood-covered gash reached clear across Charlotte's head. Karoline began screaming for her muttie and Aunt Eva to come.

When they finally found her, Karoline was lying on the ground next to the naked body of her beloved Charlotte. To this day she can't remember how long she'd been lying on the forest floor or even much of what happened. Her cousin had meant everything to her. They had shared their lives since their days of playing in the park, when they'd heard their first airplane.

The solemn, mourning group took Charlotte's body in the wagon to the nearest town where there was a cemetery. Karoline will never forget the day they buried her cousin. NEVER. It was not long before Karoline forgot how to smile…the beginning of a terrible depression which was to come.

Chapter 5: 60 Kilometers

The refugees trudged on toward Breslau through a countryside of green trees and old apple and fruit orchards…the latter a more than welcome sight whose often wormy fruit was a welcome addition to their questionable diet of the past weeks. Some of the group found bicycles on the run down farms, magnificent confiscations for the older boys who had been denied such luxuries during the past years of bombings.

Karoline's family had only a two-wheeled cart, but some of the refugees had wagons. "Mutti, are we far from home?" Karoline wanted to know. "We can't be too far, Karoline, but you know we have no idea what we'll find once we get there," she warned her daughter.

Suddenly, a truck came down the road, and Uncle Hermann immediately warned all to be aware, as they knew that it was Russian. It stopped in front of the group, and two soldiers got out. They motioned for everyone to stop, and in halting German told the mothers to let their oldest sons come with them. The mothers all tried to keep their sons with them by pleading with the men, but it was to no avail, partly because they could not understand the Russian language well enough to communicate with them.

The soldiers made the group to understand that they needed the biggest and strongest young people to help them work with the cattle drive right away. They took every child they thought strong enough to work. Many of the girls hid behind the wagons, their mothers or the people in their group. Karoline climbed inside a cart and covered herself with clothes. She shook with fear, but she needn't have worried as she was so skinny and run down at this point that the Russians wouldn't have found her useful anyway. As soon as the soldiers put the boys in their truck, they drove off. The mothers were weeping and felt most desperate, for they had no idea when they'd see their sons again.

The war was over, wasn't it? Karoline's mother couldn't help but wonder how this could happen. Their country was in such chaos. People were hungry. They had no homes, and the water was often contaminated. Nearly every day her family met someone on the road and to whom they all asked questions about their former city and their loved ones. People often said they themselves had been to Breslau and that they shouldn't go there because it was very dangerous, bombed out, and there was typhoid fever and other diseases.

Breslau was renamed Wroclaw for those people who now claimed it, and it remained in southwest Poland on either side of the Oder River. In August, 1939, Heinrich Himmler, chief of Hitler's Schutzstaffeln, wanted Polish military uniforms, which the German army procured for him. Probably neither General Halder nor any other Army commander was aware that the clothing was needed for a scheme Hitler had planned to establish an all out attack on Poland.

Between August 17 and 31, the eve of the attack, thirteen convicted criminals were taken from a concentration camp in eastern Germany to a schoolhouse to be held until his scheme was ready.

Code named "Operation Canned Goods" (the German convicts were the "goods"), the operation had two phases. In the first stage, all but one of the prisoners was ordered to dress themselves in Polish uniforms; they were given fatal injections of a drug, then taken to a small forest near Hochluinde, about 10 miles from the German-Polish border, where they were shot. Their bodies were arranged to make it appear they had died advancing into Germany, where journalists and other witnesses were brought to the scene to view the evidence of the corpses.

In the second phase of this operation, the remaining prisoner, escorted by Major Naujocks and SS members, was hustled off to Gleiwitz wearing civilian clothes and went into the radio station which they took over. One spoke in Polish and announced that Poland was attacking Germany and called all Poles to join the colors. A scuffle was simulated in front of the mike in which the prisoner was shot and left to impersonate the Polish broadcaster. At the Reichstag the next day in his speech, Hitler cited the happening at Gleiwitz as an instance of Polish aggression on German soil and said that he had thrown all the armed might of Germany against the attacking nation. World War II was launched.

Karoline watched as Mutti talked with one man she knew, Herr Scholl, and with considerable anxiety asked him if he knew anything about her Alfred.

"Mrs. Mueller, I do know that he was taken by a Russian truck, along with other men guarding the city, to a camp in Russia to work." Herr Scholl pushed the pebbles around with his shoe and looked down at the road as he talked quietly and told Emma he knew Alfred Mueller well, knew that he was a most kindly, honest man, and that he and all the others guarding the city were all put in a concentration camp at Tifles, a very pretty area in the south of Russia.

"I do not like to be the one to tell you, Frau Mueller, but we heard later that your husband died in the camp, near the town of Tifles…but please remember that we do not know this for sure. It is only what we heard." Emma could hardly look up at Herr Scholl.

"Thank you very much for telling me about Alfred, Herr Scholl," Emma said in a low voice as she turned away from the others. Of course they were not absolutely sure this news was true, so she would keep it from her girls until they knew more. A few minutes later, she turned back to Herr Scholl and the others and said she still felt drawn back to their old neighborhood, so they would have to go back and see for themselves.

Herr Scholl also told Emma of the many atrocities the people of Breslau suffered as they tried too hard, but too late to leave their city. Many women were killed by machine guns, and many young girls were raped when the Russians arrived, and they committed mass murder on those fleeing their city. Women and babies who were lucky enough were loaded into trucks and some were taken to water craft of all sizes and shapes and loaded aboard the over crowded vessels…even on the lifeboats hanging above the decks. People were desperate to flee the hated Russians.

Emma and her girls made their way carefully through Breslau's rubble-filled, cratered streets, and with much apprehension, they walked toward their old neighborhood. It was hard to recognize any place. All along the way, they picked up things in the streets that they could use when they found a place to stay. After all, nothing belonged to anyone. "Look, Mutti, here is a good pan we can use!" cried ten-year-old Ereka.

Under the overcast skies the little family tried to make the best of their terrible situation while looking at the torn up city which had been their home. The girls decided to make a game of it and said to Emma, "It's just like Christmas when we find things, Mutti," and Karoline wondered to herself if they would ever have their live pine tree, all decorated with candles, again.

She thought of the exciting customs of Dec. 24, 25 and 26. Mutti and Vater always decorated the beautiful, green, wonderfully scented pine tree and lit the candles before she and Ereka could see it! How they oohed and awed over its brilliance. Then they sang Christmas carols until the candles burned out. The next night they used new candles and did the same. *Will we ever get back to such wonderful times again?* she wondered.

They found a cup and even some utensils before they came upon an apartment house still standing. They were the first to come upon it, so they proclaimed it their new home! They went up to the third floor where they not only felt safer, but found living quarters with two rooms. Someone had left a table, two chairs and a mattress. There was an old stove in the corner of the room, but there was nothing to burn in it, so they went down to the street to hunt for wood or whatever would burn so they could keep warm.

They found some broken furniture strewn near the railroad tracks, so they loaded all the scraps they could into the small wagon they found back of the apartment. Herr Japes, who had once been a neighbor, was also hunting for wood scraps and began helping them. He showed them how to get torf, a marsh material which was cut in pieces, dried on one side, then turned over to dry on the other before it was ready to use. He also helped them find animal chips laying in the streets and gave them helpful, much needed advice on safety measures to ward off diseases.

Every day, the refugees who had returned from the mountains worked hard to pick up the rubble, load it into wagons and push the debri to dumping areas. There was no pay. There was no one to pay them. They just wanted to clean up their city. Sore backs and muscles weren't considerations. They were alive! Of course the Polish people living in "their" city were happy to see such effort.

Even finding the beautiful, mahogany furniture with legs broken and one dining chair nearby didn't make it easier for Emma and the girls to burn them. But the most important consideration of all was how they would get food. Karoline went with her mutti to a Polish worker's kitchen, a cafeteria where they served around 300 workers and where the girl would get her own food and bring home ANY table scraps or leftovers she could find. She got no money, just her food. Emma sewed pockets into her daughter's underclothing in which she could stash whatever food she could find. It didn't matter if it was off someone else's plate. They had to have food to stay alive.

The cook, a greasy, heavyset Pole who managed the cafeteria for the Polish workers, liked Karoline. She wondered how much she could smuggle out in her pockets without getting caught. She could not take a chance on losing this job. It would mean starvation for all.

Mr. Lubawa, the butcher, would sometimes give Karoline a piece of fresh meat to take home…but never without his demands for a kiss and sometimes a smothering, frightening squeeze. Often he would wait until she came through the kitchen doors with both hands full. If no one was near, he would brush close to her in his dirty, once-white apron and put his hands where he shouldn't. Karoline began to worry about where she could be to avoid his advances.

One day a Polish lady came to their apartment. "I want your apartment. You will have to move!" she announced firmly to them. Breslau was now a Polish city, Wroclaw, and they were the beaten Germans. There was nothing they could do but look for another place to live. They found one, but the drawback was that the toilet was down the hall and you had to pull a long cord to flush it. But it did work, and they felt lucky to find new living quarters.

"What have you for us tonight, Karoline?" Ereka would squeal when her sister came home from work. Mutti was always just as excited. The three of them would sit on what furniture they had and thoroughly enjoy the delicious scraps Karoline was able to bring as they chattered about the happenings of the day.

"Today I found more yarn in the street, Karoline, and I'm knitting you and Ereka warm socks. The things I made last week Ereka is selling for Polish money." Because of her age, Ereka could sit out on the street to sell, but Karoline would have been stolen by the Russians had she tried the same.

One morning as Karoline was leaving for work, a truck full of Polish soldiers stopped in front of her and ordered her to get in. She was terrified. They made her understand that they would not harm her. They were picking up women and girls to help them clean and peel potatoes! They turned out to be just happy guys who wanted to talk and sing with them! They instructed the women to clean the latrines and took Karoline and the other young girls into the kitchen where they played the harmonica, sang and laughed all day as the girls peeled potatoes. This very thing happened to Karoline twice, but she felt it was something that would make her mutti worry too much, so she didn't tell her.

Karoline also worked at another job where a young Russian soldier, Boris, with a pretty blond wife and baby, was her boss. Between his Jewish friend and him, they kept their young German girl busy cleaning their houses. In this way, their pretty slave would help PAY for what her country had done to them.

One day she was helping with Annagret and Boris' baby, Hanns, and had put him down for his nap, when she heard someone coming up the stairs. It was Boris. He was coming home early. Karoline put her hands over her mouth and gasped. She was alone. He uneasy feeling made her shiver as she tried to get out of the room, but he blocked her way. Try as she might, she couldn't get past him. The young father grabbed her and threw her on the bed. "I don't do that!!" she cried, as she tried to pull her skirt down and fought him with all her strength to get his smelly hands and body off of her. He was already moaning with the pleasure he felt was sure to come. Karoline thought of what her mutti had told her and was afraid he would hit her, when they heard footsteps running up the stairs. Boris thought it was his wife, so he let go of a crying, shaking Karoline in disgust. Emma and the girls needed what little money she was earning in her cleaning job, so how could she tell mutti what had happened? She would tell her some other untruth that would allow her to quit working for the Russian.

But there was still the Jewish boy, Samuel, to think about. He had been very nice to her, and they had had a few dates when he started to get too serious, so Karoline hid when he came. She told her mutti, "You must tell him I'm not here and get rid of him! Just tell him I'm not at home, mutti...please!" Emma knew her daughter sounded desperate so did as her daughter asked her.

They had been living there awhile when there was a knock at the Meuller's door. Emma was surprised to find a Polish soldier and his female companion standing there. In halting German, he told her they needed a place to sleep that night and wanted to use her bed. Emma had no choice. She let the two in. *Would they always have to pay for their government's terrible folly?* she wondered.

"I will bring you some food for supper, and you can cook for all of us," he promised. Though Emma doubted his word, she said nothing. Much later when he reappeared with plenty of food for all of them that evening, she smiled warmly and said, "Danke, danke" and was more than happy to cook for everyone. The meal was so good, and the room was filled with laughter and much talking, but with little understanding of what was said!

It wasn't long before the Polish people told the Germans they wanted them out. "This is our city now. You have to leave! You must either become Polish citizens or be ready to leave in an hour's notice by train."

"Where will we go? Where are you sending us?" they asked in sadness and fear.

"You will be sent into your country toward the west," the man speaking told them.

Emma, Karoline and Ereka began to wonder if their lives could ever be happy again.

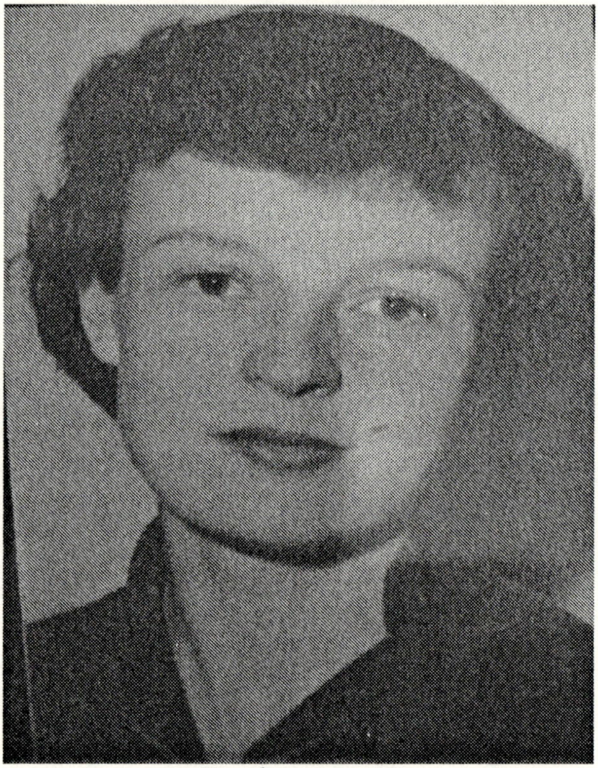

Karoline (age 19)

Chapter 6: Refugees Go West

It was winter in Breslau. Their former, large, industrial city would now be known as Poland's Wroclaw. The Polish people in charge blew whistles and moved to the railway station to get the Germans to queue up for their climbing into the boxcars, the vichwaggons which had carried cattle, troops to the front and Jews to holding camps, labor camps or ghettos. "You will be taken far into western Germany to a larger city where you car will be dropped off. That is where you will get out and people will meet you and give you a place to live." The Polish people in charge gave each person some herring and bread and told them it might take ten days for them to find their city.

Karoline, her mother, little sister, Aunt Eva and family had no desire to become Polish citizens, so they climbed into a car which was littered with dirt, papers and had a large barrel in the center of the floor which was covered with a warped board. That was their relief barrel. There was some straw on the floor, and though there were no lights, the large cracks between some of the boards let in a tiny bit of light.

Karoline sat down as close to the big doors as she could so she could be among the first of the twenty or more emigrants to get out when the train made one of its periodic stops. She pulled as hard as she could on her old black coat to get it over her ankles to keep her legs warmer and watched her mutti and little sister find a place to sit next to the inside wall. Ereka was crying. Her mutti was holding her tightly and rocking her. *How would they stay alive?* Karoline wondered.

This seventeen-year-old German girl had known no other way of life, only that of what she and all her friends had gone through—war and bombings. Hitler's Nazi party, the disappearance of all her Jewish friends and teachers, 'round the clock bombings and bomb shelters, where she'd spent so many hours. One ray of sunshine was the mandatory joining into the Hitler Youth. Both sexes joined. Girls from 10 years of age met every week, where they sang wonderful songs, hiked, danced, dressed in navy skirts and white blouses and had other instruction from their leaders. They were the League of German Girls. Hitler's male youth were trained both mentally and physically. They were toughened in service for the Reich, and Karoline's little friend from her early park days, Freidrick, was one of them. Herr Japes had seen Freidrick on one of his visits in Breslau and was told how the youth helped harvest crops, camped in the forests, sang and exercised as one! There were hours of drilling with emphasis on a group rather than an individual, which meant they would someday fight as a team for Hitler. These groups enjoyed many competitions, and sometimes the winners would be fortunate enough to meet their Fuhrer! These youngsters worshiped him and would never stop fighting for him.

The Hitler Youth were trained in different branches; some in the Marine Youth, which resorted in their sailing the Danube or training aboard a navy vessel; the Motor Youth, who became skillful with their motorcycles, including learning to repair them; and the youth in the air branch, who built model airplanes, possibly enjoyed a flight in a bomber or fighter or got to take off in a glider. If the youth showed unusually high promise, they were sent to special schools to eventually learn to be leaders of the Reich, and parents were told they had no right to refuse their youngster's attendance to such schools with such rigorous screening. The Hitler Youth leaders began to teach 1.5 million boys how to shoot during its first year with guns. They were all learning the military basics needed for Hitler's future armies, and even preteenagers were taught antiaircraft defense.

The disappearance of her father and the death of her best friend were her saddest memories. Karoline put her head against the rattling vichwaggon and tried to block out such happenings of her life. She needed to go, but to use the big, smelly barrel in the center of the car that she hated, Emma had to hold an old coat around her for a little privacy. The barrel sloshed over its lid covering when the train rumbled.

Karoline had had no shoes of her own for a very long time, but her mutti and little sister had dug through piles of old shoes in the rubbles of Breslau and were lucky enough to find some small, black, worn, men's shoes that fit her. "Now I can walk better, and my feet won't be so cold!" Karoline said as she laughed aloud. To herself in a most reverent silence, she thanked her God for his help. She cared not at all that her "new" shoes had once belonged to a man.

Emma had knit socks for her girls from the yarn they'd found in the street and also some mittens for Ereka to sell for what Polish money she could get. Ereka, at about ten years of age, was young enough that she could sit in front of their building and sell items and not worry about the soldiers picking her up, but Karoline, at 16, would not have dared to sit at the street because the Polish soldiers would stop in their trucks and make her get in.

The old engine belched white steam skyward as it pulled the freight cars (vichwaggons) westward far into Germany. The refugees were crammed into the boxcars. Karoline would try to wait until the train made one of its few stops so that she could relieve herself back of some bushes. Her feet were so cold she wondered how she'd be able to stand, as her coat wasn't quite long enough to cover her legs and reach to the straw-covered boards. She would wait.

The herring and bread the Polish people had given them when they pulled away from the station wouldn't last these hungry people long. Karoline's whole body ached from the cold. Suddenly, as if the old car felt her misery, it ceased the constant, fast chatter, and the heavy wheels changed their rhythm. They were slowing down. KKKSSSHSSH! came from the steam engine, then came the final jerk. Nothing. They could hear nothing. They waited. Then muffled sounds of doors sliding open came from the car in front of them.

They held their breaths and hardly moved until they heard the iron bolts slide open with much grinding and screeching from the rusty hinges. Sharp winds blew into the already cold boxcar. The hungry refugees tried to stand and shaded their eyes from the glare of the morning sunlight. It was thin sunlight, but their eyes had become accustomed to near darkness. There was much talk among the exiting, weary emigrants who were murmuring about seeing the outside world.

How wonderful it was to see the countryside, even in the short December days, Karoline thought. It made her smile. That smile made her cold, reddened face feel funny. She shaded her hazel eyes, framed by thick, dark lashes and brushed back her tangled, curly brown hair with her hand so she could see farther off into the distance. Karoline could tell they were a short way from a small town. Slowly the emigrants clamored down to stretch their legs and make welcome trips into the bushes.

"Karoline, please hurry right back," Emma called as her daughter ran to the rows of thick shrubbery near the tracks.

"I will hurry, Mutti!" the girl said as she stumbled through the frozen clods of dirt beside the tracks to hunt for seclusion from the others. It was so stressful and made her even colder to raise her skirt in the cold air and still keep a close watch for anyone coming.

It wasn't long before Emma came up to her daughter holding Ereka by the hand. Emma said, "They will not drop our car off here, but they might drop off Aunt Eva's. Hurry, we must get back out of the cold."

They walked quickly back and forth in their car to keep warm until the whistle shrieked and the steam began to rise. Their train began to head farther west, and the Mueller's car was near the front so to be one of the last cars to be dropped off. "That was Aunt Eva's car that was just dropped off," Emma said sadly to her girls. "Do not worry, someday we will see them again," she said in her most positive voice. "The man said we were between east and west Germany and would be close to Hampschter when we stop tomorrow." Karoline thought her mutti sounded happier with this statement than any time during their days of rail travel.

But what Emma didn't tell her girls was what had happened to Aunt Eva's car during the night. While their boxcar was shunted to the side of the tracks to make way for other trains to pass, young Polish boys entered and robbed the refugees of anything that had been missed in Breslau.

"We have nothing left, Emma," cried Eva.

"Just think what has happened to some of the others and be thankful," came Emma's reply.

Earlier reports had been of cars parked overnight in rail stations on the siding when Polish bandits not only robbed their victims but took the women into the station to violate them. It was then that Eva agreed with her sister before she said goodbye. "We *will* meet again soon, won't we, Emma?"

Just as they reached the vichwaggon, an old, crippled farmer in overalls, who probably lived near the apple orchard she could see in the distance, shuffled slowly up to them, and they could tell it was he who had labored so to open their big, heavy doors. He smiled at them. Karoline knew he must live nearby, possibly in that old, dilapidated farmhouse near the tracks, and he gave them a warm German greeting; "Wie gehts!" he called, and they answered the same, "Wie gehts!" Then, to her surprise he reached under the big, heavy box he'd used as their step and picked up a container of water and big chunks of dark bread. Karoline drew in her breath and let out a loud gasp.

"Mutti, look!" she cried as she put her hands to her quivering lips. She laughed aloud and felt a surge of more happiness than she'd known for a long time. "MUTTI, Ereka!! Come!" she yelled as the old man offered the heavy, straw basket's contents to the refugees, but to Karoline first. They all accepted the bread with great surges of "danka, danka, danka!!"and put their bounty inside their ragged coat pockets. The heavy basket was full to the brim of the prettiest, fattest, red apples, great hunks of yellow cheese and big, ragged pieces of dark, freshly baked, rye bread! Karoline's cold hands grabbed at the food as if it would get away from her. She stopped. *There it was again*, she thought to herself again. *God answered my prayers!*

"Will you please take just one of each so there will be some for everyone?" the farmer asked, in a hoarse, husky voice.

"Is he God, Mutti??" the hungry girl asked in a whisper to her smiling mother.

"Danke!! Danke!!! You have saved our lives!" they all yelled as they made their way back to the waiting car and waved to their wonderful savior! The shrillness of the whistle pierced the countryside as steam shot upward through the cold winter air. Karoline couldn't help looking back toward that wonderful, old man as long as the doors were open. They were saved from starving, and they were leaving once again.

Before she dared enjoy her coming meal, Karoline looked around to get her eyes accustomed to where her mutti and sister were huddled together. She tried to get her feet under her legs for warmth and pulled her worn, black coat clear down to the straw to hold her body heat before she attacked this heaven-sent bread. "Karoline, you must chew a long time and eat very slowly," Mutti had warned her. "We can't have stomachaches." It was the most delicious bread she'd ever tasted. Oh, how she loved that sweet, old farmer, even though he'd been so slow closing their big doors! She felt she could forgive him for anything and thanked her God.

She chewed slowly, savoring every bite, and thought of where they'd be dropped off and where they'd live, and how they'd live. The man in Breslau had said, "Each boxcar would be dropped off at a different town, and you'll have to find people there to help you. That is where you will live!"

Karoline let her tears flow. Who could see her in the twilight, anyway? She didn't want anyone to see her crying, and maybe now, with her tummy full, she would have a wonderful dream of their next home!

Chapter 7: A New Life

It was a cold month of December, 1946, and Karoline was still feeling the affects of leaving Bresslau, the capital of the province on either side of the Oder River. In 1945 about 68% of the city was destroyed. The Germans had defended their city for about three months but many blocks of houses were demolished in the older sector so that an airstrip could be built there, and Russian heavy artillary did the rest. Two gothic churches, St. Elizabeth and St. Mary Magdalon near the market square, dated from the 13th century were damaged but later repaired.

To the south are the Sudetens, a mountain range and popular tourist area with mineral springs and health resorts. This was a large coal producing area, and there were deposits of copper, granite, basalt, sandstone and much agriculture in the lowlands and large wooded areas about ¼ of the province.

Karoline was now 17, and had chosen her bed of straw as close to the wide, wooden doors of the dilapidated vichwaggon as she could get so that when they made one of their periodic stops, she could be out first. Though she almost always kept her feelings to herself, she couldn't help the hate and inner rage she felt knowing what these cars had hauled before she and the other displaced countrymen had been put in them.

With a careless, sweeping gesture, Karoline shoved her long, dark, matted hair off her face. How long had it been since she'd seen a comb? There were none to buy, but sometimes they'd been lucky enough to find one in the rubble of the streets of bombed out Breslau.

The clickety clack of the wheels on the rails was monotonous. It made her drowsy, but the constant motion of the freight made the stench from the slopping, big bucket worse and sleeping nearly impossible.

The cracks in the walls of the old boxcar occasionally let in enough light for Karoline to catch a quick glimpse of her mutti and frail, 11-year-old Ereka huddled against a wall. Her sister was scarcely able to cope with more suffering. Tangled, brown hair lay matted to her tear-stained, somber face. Mutti was holding and rocking her youngest daughter who was oscillating between moaning and crying as she tried to catch sight of Karoline.

"God, please help us," Emma prayed softly, as she tried to hold back her tears. She had been brought up in a strict Lutheran faith, but had married Alfred Mueller who was Catholic. Both families had found their beliefs difficult to mix at times, but Emma made sure that her girls had always attended church, and they believed in prayer.

Karoline could see her breath in the cold car and listened to the shrill whistle shriek as it split the winter air. With her eyes closed, she could imagine the steam shooting skyward.

Through the cracks she could see snow on the ground and knew they were in the country. Naked trees framed barren, brown fields and only a few houses appeared in the grey, dismal distance. The smoke that curled lazily skyward from those chimneys gave the young girl a feeling of yearning, yearning for the home and happy life she barely remembered. Slowly, she moved her cramped, cold legs to a new position.

Amidst the broken trees near the busy railroad tracks and across the fields she could see a few jagged buildings still standing. The gravel road was strewn with wrecked army trucks and other heavy equipment she couldn't identify. This scene brought back memories of the 'round-the-clock bombings of Breslau and the many times the sirens had sounded which sent them to the shelters with their arms filled with anything they could carry to help while away the hours spent there.

Suddenly the clickety clack sounds grew farther apart. Were they slowing down? Karoline hoped they'd be stopping and she could get out to relieve herself. Maybe now she wouldn't have to use the barrel. Suddenly, as if the old car felt her misery, it ceased its constant fast chatter and the heavy wheels changed their tone. The Vichwaggon was slowing down with a KKKSHHH KKKSHSH coming from the steam engine before it came to its final jerking stop. Everyone waited quietly for someone to come and lift the heavy metal arm and shove the weathered, wooden doors open. It was hard to see at first until their eyes adjusted to even the dull light of the winter day, but it was even harder to stand.

It was a bitter, cold, grey day with clouds rushing across the sky. It was early afternoon when the engine's shrill whistle blasted the thick winter air twice to announce their arrival in HELMSTED!! Steam billowed high above the freight. It had taken ten days to reach this city and their food, in spite of the wonderful farmers en route, had not lasted that long. The refugees were cold, stiff and hungry.

Several men were standing near their car as the emigrants looked out the open door. Karoline saw jagged buildings, broken trees and ugly big craters in the land. It didn't matter to her. They had finally arrived!! Everyone was excited, and low murmurs filled with happy sounds of anticipation were more than evident. It had been many days since Karoline had heard this kind of excitement.

Those in charge of directing the refugees waited patiently for all to disembark. The young men seemed friendly enough, and even offered help to those who found it hard to walk, but to trust any male now was difficult for Karoline, though she said nothing, even if they WERE German. Her large, hazel, sad eyes showed little mutual expression to the smiling faces of the young men as she forced a weak smile and a "danka, danka," to them.

"Pitte, follow me" one of them said as he led the straggling group to a building set up to take care of them. The leader, in a raunchy, little hat, said, pointing, "The men will line up here, and the women will be over there. Everyone must shower in that building before being de-liced. You MUST be de-liced whether you have lice or not. That is not a question! Please get into your lines," he said louder, so that he might be heard above the murmuring and embarrassed whispers coming from some of the group.

"Following your de-licing, you will go to that building for soup," he added, pointing and smiling broadly. He knew their hunger. Then came words of joy and much excited chatter as they emitted more words of "Danke! Danke!"

"Please, go to your showers now and come back here after you have enjoyed them. You will remain here for three days before you take another train to Lohne, your new home!" he added, smiling.

Karoline and Ereka were understandably amazed that there were *hot showers*, and their mother stood by them as the three kept one shower busy. How long had it been? To their great amazement, there was a much later model toilet than she had ever seen. "Look, Mutti, a *white toilet!* You push this," she whispered excitedly. "Isn't it wonderful?" she chirped, as she told Ereka just to wait her turn. "There's even newspaper!"

Back outside the building, they stood once more in line. Mutti said in a low voice, "Stand here, Karoline. You must raise your dress for this." Karoline was quiet. She looked at her mutti for security before she said, "Yes, mutti, I will," in a small voice obviously filled with quiet exasperation. When they were ready for her she kept her eyes on the ground. She simply could not look at the men with their de-licing guns.

The heavenly aroma of potato with ham soup permeated the winter air and sharpened her senses to such a point her mouth weatered. *First, hot showers and now hot soup?* It was such a turning point in her bleak life that she wasn't sure she could handle without crying. She no longer cared that she had had to go through the embarrassment of de-licing when they were treated this kindly! She'd forgotten what color potato and ham soup was and definitely how it tasted! Then the smell of freshly baked bread nearly made her faint. Was this Heaven?

The refugees enjoyed hard mattresses, the washroom and food for three days before they were put on a train to Lohne, which was in the province of Oldenberg. "How can we stand such a wonderful life, Mutti?" she whispered to her smiling mother.

Their train was not the miserable boxcar but one much better than the vichwaggon they had arrived at Hampschter in. They listened with apprehension to the shrill whistle of the engine as it began to move toward their final destination of Lohne. What would life bring them Karoline began to wonder?

When the whistle's shrill sound pierced the air Emma, Ereka and Karoline strained to see out the dirty windows. Emma was very nervous. Would someone come to them when they got off the train? What would she and her girls do if they didn't? The doors opened, and the three of them pushed closer together as all the emigrants went down the iron steps toward the platform. There were many people at the depot. Everyone walked away from the train and began to look for someone, who they did not know. There was lots of talking, some laughing and much standing back just to watch. A couple with a little baby in their arms moved closer to Emma and her girls. They stood back and looked at each other until the husband said to them, "We are looking for people to stay with us. We want to share our home with them, and they can help us with the work, and we will have food for us all. Emma looked at the mother and baby, and they all offered their hands and smiles as Frau Blaschke and Herr Blaschke picked them to come home with them. "We just have a small home, but we will make room for you," Frau Blaschke said to Emma.

"Do you have a place to go?" Herr Blaschke asked Emma.

"Nein!" Emma replied as she looked longingly at the baby son.

"Come!" said Herr Blaschke. "We will take you to our home."

Emma, Karoline and Ereka couldn't believe such a God-given offer…a chance to be in a home!! Frau Blaschke showed them to a bedroom just for them and at once made them feel just like family. They had little, but Emma would be eternally grateful to them for their willingness to share. It wasn't long before she happily helped with little Fritz and started to cook for the family. Emma sang as she worked; she was *so* happy.

Within two days of their arrival in Lohne, Karoline got her first real job with pay! She was hired to sew for a boutique where they taught her to make dolls. There were other girls, some about her age, also working in the small factory, and she soon made friends. The girls soon began to eat their lunches together, and within a few weeks, they started to go to the Sunday night dances in Lohne.

The teenagers of Germany were now dancing to the same tunes as those in the United States were enjoying. Glen Miller! There was "In

The Mood," "Jersey Bounce," "Boogie Woogi," Sentimental Journey" and many others.

One early evening Karoline waited in line to get into the dance hall with her girl friend. Just as suddenly as a rain squall might appear, a tall, redheaded boy approached her. "Here's your ticket!" he said as he looked into her eyes. "Will you get us a table? I will be right back." Karoline just looked at him. She didn't even have time to answer. He was gone up ahead into the crowd. Ilse had just come back, and they looked at each other quizzically. "What should I do?" Karoline asked Ilse.

"You go in and get your table, and I will see you later."

Karoline did as she was told, but she just wasn't used to this and wondered if he'd return. She found an empty table near the dance floor, but was too embarrassed to look around for him, and began to wonder after a few minutes if she should leave. Maybe he's playing a trick on me; then what should I do was foremost in her mind. She was about to lay her sweater on the chair next to her when Gustov Karl came swaggering up.

"Vell, gut!" he exclaimed as a broad smile of white teeth greeted her. "Ve vill dance!" She couldn't conceal her embarrassment as she lowered her pretty, dark head of curls and said softly, "I am Karoline Mueller, and I don't know *how* to dance!" she said as she looked into those green eyes.

"Don't vorry. I vill teach you, " he said excitedly. Before she could even think of objecting, he pulled her up onto the dance floor. He was all muscle, and she felt weak all over. The firm way he held her made her shivver. She couldn't help but follow his lead as he took smooth, easy steps. She couldn't believe she could dance; but they danced, danced and danced. Everyone around them simply seemed like blurrs to her. Her feet ached, but they just kept on dancing!

Finally she got so tired she ran out of breath and gathered courage enough to ask him shyly if they could please sit down for awhile. "Vell, you sit, and I vill get us some of my favorite beer," he said eagerly. But Karoline was so excited and so very tired that she told Gustov she was needed at home in just a half hour, so she would have to leave, as her mother was not feeling well.

He sat down next to her and looked right into her eyes and started to ask her questions. "Where are you from?" he wanted to know. When she said Breslau and told him it was no longer that, he leaned forward and asked her how they got here. Karoline was getting nervous. But he wanted to know more, so as he took big gulps of his favorite beer, Karoline decided she couldn't stay any longer. "I vill valk you home," he said sorrowfully, "and maybe we can walk tomorrow, yaw?"

The next evening, at home, she waited by the window with her mutti until she saw him coming up the road. "Mutti, that is the man I'm going to marry!" she said with eyes shining as they never had before. Mutti watched as the young German walked briskly up their road.

Gustov's red, fine hair was blowing in the early evening breeze as he met Karoline on the front porch and shook Emma's hand. He told Emma he was happy to meet her, and said pleasantly, "I vill bring Karoline home early, Mrs. Mueller."

They walked down a long lane near a bubbling stream and talked of small things before sitting beside the bank for awhile. Gustov asked Karoline to tell him about her life in Breslau. It made her feel embarrassed to talk so much about herself, but he was easy to talk to, so she told him about her life until she went to the mountains. It was hard for her to tell him about Charlotte, and she started to cry. "Ve vill talk more another time," he said with such understanding that they got up and walked to a store where they sold sodas before. Then Gustov walked her home.

"I vill come for you tomorrow, yah?"

Karoline went to their apartment and up to her mutti's bedroom. With eyes shining she told her mother how she'd enjoyed being with this outgoing young man. "He's fun, Mutti…he laughs a lot," she said as they sat on Emma's bed. Emma wasn't feeling well, but Karoline told her that Gustov was coming for her after work again the day after tomorrow.

It was Sunday, and they were lucky enough to get another table near the dance floor. They sat down to have Gustov's favorite beer. He wanted to hear more about her life, so to get away from the music and laughter, they took their beer out onto the porch.

There were times she started to shake when she told Gustov things she couldn't believe she was telling someone she'd only recently met! *How could she feel that she had known him for such a long time?* she wondered.

Gustov listened with intense interest and said, "I just vas in the medics, but I learned to shoot artillary ven I vas sixteen. Ve tried to shoot the planes down! My English is not so good because Hitler told us everyone vill be talking German anyway. Now I vill tell you of my family's bad time, yah?"

(Because Gustov and Karoline decided to speak German, which was their lifelong language, I will not use his fractured English.)

I was away during the last of the war when my mother and two sisters were staying in a farmhouse near the Russian border. (Gustov's parents had run a clothing store and had taught him to be a master tailor).

"One night when they were going to have supper, my mother heard heavy footsteps coming onto the porch. It was very dark, and they couldn't see out, but she could tell there was more than one person. They were stomping their feet. 'Helene…Marriana…run…you hide! *Don't* come out…you understand?!' Everyone had heard how the Russians were treating German girls.

"My mother knew what they wanted. And there was no one around to protect them. My mother was a very strong woman, but she couldn't hold off many soldiers. The pounding started. The men yelled for her to open the door as they pounded louder. They were speaking Russian, but it was so easy for her to catch enough words that her heart made her thin wash dress and sweater jump. She didn't know what to do. If she answered, they would know she was a woman, but of course everyone knew the men were away at war," Gustov said gesturing futilely with his hands as he continued his story.

"She had to make the right decision, so she started to pray…harder than she'd ever prayed in her life to save my sisters, and she knew the only way was to give them what they wanted and hope Helene and

Marianna had found good enough hiding places.

"'There is no one here but me, and I'm an old woman,' she yelled, trying to sound very hoarse. They pounded harder and began to yank on the rusty, metal knob. She didn't answer the door. There was a pause, then she heard them talking to each other. They rammed their shoulders against the door, and she knew they wouldn't stop, but would force their way in. 'All right...I let you in,' she yelled. Pushing and shoving, about 18 dirty, big, smelly Russian soldiers stormed in jabbering and laughing.

"She was sure they were asking where the others were because they gestured to the three place settings on the table. Her hand went to her mouth, but she acted like she didn't understand. She kept shaking her head, saying, 'I am alone.' They laughed and pushed her against the wall. The leader with the big teeth and bad breath ripped her dress and shoved her down to the floor. She landed hard. All of them began laying their guns on the table and the leader motioned for another to watch them as they started pulling down their pants. My mother landed so hard her braids fell down and she couldn't help but cry out. The men just laughed harder," Gustov said, and his face twisted with emotion. "'I will give you what you want,' she told them, hoping they'd stay in the room with her. They shoved her back down and tore off all her clothes except her socks and shoes and attacked her brutally, each one.

"When Helene and Marianna heard their mother's cries as she hit the floor they came running out to help her. 'Mutti...Mutti, leave our mutti alone!' they yelled as they tried to reach the guns on the table.

"'Go back...run away!' my mother said to them. Seeing two young girls sent the men in a frenzy! Immediately, two would hold my sisters while the others ripped off their clothes. The girls screamed. They cried hysterically and yelled to the men to stop! Helene's fierce kicking made her attacker so angry he took her into the bedroom and threw her onto the bed. His comrads came to help. Sobbing frantically, she still fought them. 'Please don't hurt me!' she begged through her tears. Her dark hair flew across her wet eyelashes as they brutally landed blows to her head. When one blow hit too hard, she knew nothing more. She didn't feel their thrusts. Their laughing and moaning were no longer felt by the unconscious German girl.

"Marianna lay sobbing on the bedroom floor as all the men took their turns. Blood was everywhere. They knocked my mother out when she tried to get up to help my sisters. She had fought as hard as she could, but it was no use," Gustov added as the tears slid down his cheeks.

Karoline was crying too, as it took her back to those painful memories of Charlotte in the forest. She put her slender hand on top of his and looked into his sad eyes. Gustov tried to regain his composure. "My mother, her name is Gertrude Karl, the next thing she heard was birds chirping outside the windows. She tried to move. Her bruised arms slipped in pools of blood. In the dim, early morning light, she couldn't see past the bedroom door. The banging in her ears made it hard to hear when she called to the girls as she pulled her aching body toward the bedroom.

"Marianna, sobbing quietly, was doubled up in a corner with her arms around her legs. She was shivering with cold, and dried blood covered her legs. Ripped, stained clothes were strewn across the floor. Helene lay on the bed, naked except for her socks. She was not moving and was very cold. My mother covered her, and she and Marianna rubbed Helene for a long time as they talked to her trying to get her warm. Finally, my sister opened her eyes.

"As soon as Helene was able to walk, a day or two later, my mother started their long walk to the hospital. Helene needed medical help. Along the road, to keep them away, she had to yell at the soldiers who came near. 'My daughter has syphllis!' My mother had only guessed this, but she said it to save Helene from further molestation. But it turned out to be true.

"The hospital told her that Helene would have to be sent to a special sanitarium that would help her. My mother prayed. When she went to the sanitarium to visit Helene, the person in charge told her how sorry they were. Helene had died of complications. My mother's prayers didn't help. She never prayed again. She said, 'There is NO God!'"

Gustov walked Karoline home, and in the ensuing days, they met often. Three days later, when Karoline came home from work, the lady in the next apartment met her at the door and told her to come quickly. "You mama is sick," she said with great concern in her voice. "She fell on the stairway this afternoon, and we put her to bed, but she has been calling for you, Karoline!"

Karoline ran up the stairs to her mutti's bed. "Mutti...what is it...what is wrong?" She grabbed her sick mother and held her tightly in her arms as the tears streamed down her face. Emma looked very white, and her long, dark hair, usually in a neat bun, looked as though it had never been combed. She looked up at her daughter with glazed, hollow-looking eyes, and Karoline knew she was very ill.

"Karoline, you and Ereka must live with Aunt Sophia if I don't get better. Promise me. She will take care of you."

"NO, Mutti. NO...No, don't leave me!! Please!!!" she said through her tears. "I don't like Aunt Sophia! The sobbing girl held her mutti as tightly as she could. She rocked her. It wasn't until then that Karoline realized how thin and weak her mutti was. Emma died in Karoline's arms.

Chapter 8: The Danish Red Cross

Aunt Sophia and her husband, Siegfried, Ereka and Karoline's father's brother's wife, arrived to take over the care of Ereka. Karoline was now 19, and her depression worsened. There were four people and one bed, but her aunt and uncle just moved right in and took over the apartment. Ereka, now 11, had become more frail and weak, and Karoline couldn't seem to recuperate from the loss of her mother. She became despondent. She woke up one day and couldn't swallow, so they sent her to a hospital for three days.

When Gustov came to see her, he said, "Karoline, you must talk to your pastor." His name was Pastor Stachbart, from their Lutheran Church, and he had been their pastor long enough to know the girls well. Karoline began to cry. She could NOT stop. She wanted to die.

Pastor Stachbart told her she could not stay in the house with her aunt and uncle, but Ereka could stay there and he would help her. "I will contact the Danish Red Cross and see what they can do," he said to her.

Pastor Stachbart was told Karoline should be sent to a sanitarium in Germany for a short time. "Karoline, it is like a school where you will be cared for and have your own duties and studies. It is in a quiet mountain setting, and I feel you need the rest, as your nerves cannot take any more," the kindly pastor told her.

Gustov came to see her the next day. "Gustov, should I go?" she asked him. He had been such a good friend, and he was the only person she felt she could talk to.

Gustov looked into her sad, hazel eyes and said quietly, "Karoline, I want you to go. I will write to you, and I will come to see you," he said as tears slid down his cheeks and he reached for her cold hand.

Karoline went, with the help of dear Pastor Stachbart.

"You will be fine with Aunt and Uncle, Ereka, and I will see you as soon as I feel better." She arrived at the Salzgitter, a former glider school in the Hartz Mountains of Germany.

Karoline was frightened, but more than that, she was lonely…that awful feeling again. On the way to the school, she thought of the stories her oma once told her and Charlotte. Weren't they about the witches astride their brooms on Mt. Brocken? It was her inner self talking…you will have to get such things out of your mind. Enough is enough. Karoline closed her eyes, leaned her head back against her seat and decided her life would have to become more happy since it would now be free of tragedy.

The room she was assigned to was clean, but small, and it had a window facing the mountains where she could see the deep blue line of trees in the forest as they climbed higher up the mountain, then began to thin out. She sat down at her desk in the straight backed chair and put her head down. There was a barely discernible knock on her door, so she wiped her eyes before going to answer it. A nice looking lady in a white uniform was there and said, "I am your teacher, Karoline, and my name is Greta. This girl is your special helper and will be your friend," she said as she smiled brightly and reached for Karoline's hand. "Her name is Ingrid." Karoline tried her best to greet them, and she thought how pretty Ingrid was, but she felt her stomach churning as she put her hand out to the two of them.

They told her the sanitarium housed 49 others who had been through more than they could bear and were from the ages of 17 to 21. It seemed to Karoline to be a very pleasant place.

"The duties of you girls includes schedules of running the beautiful, quiet, mountain trails at 6:00 AM; showering at 6:30AM; going to breakfast with everyone in the dining area then carrying out assigned chores such as washing dishes, washing and mending clothes and ironing. Following this, there will be two hours of classes," Greta explained.

Karoline enjoyed the morning runs on the dewy mountain paths, but sometimes she thought of the fairytales oma (her grandmother) had told her and then tended to follow the other girls more closely! In a few days she felt a little more relaxed and was looking forward to a visit from her good friend who had written her.

He would stay in an ajoining dormitory for several days and be invited to join everyone for dinner. He would sit beside Karoline, which pleased her very much. She had been thinking about him and had made up her mind to get well as fast as possible so they could see each other more. "Ingrid, I can't tell you how much he has helped me, and I don't want to lose him, like I did my mutti and my papa," she said, with tears in her eyes, to her special friend and nurse. "I will help you all I can," Ingrid assured her.

The long tables were covered with white cloths, and all the visitors were asked to stand and be introduced. This was especially hard for Karoline, but Gustov, who was sitting next to her, always came to her rescue! She thought how much his personality was like that of her mutti, happy and so outgoing, and how she wanted to be more like that!

When Karoline went to her room one night, she thought of the terrible times when they had had no food and she would have to bring home scraps just so they could stay alive. Her new life was a dream come true, and it made her shudder and want to pinch herself to see if it was real! Once more, she thanked her wonderful God!

From May until the fall, Karoline stayed in these pleasant surroundings and slowly recovered her strength. Ingrid said, "You are strong enough to leave here now, Karoline, but my parents would like you to come to our home near Copenhagen and become part of our family for six months. They will come for you if you would like to do that...would you?"

Ingrid had become a wonderful friend and had been at her side as a nurse and advisor for these first six months in the sanitarium. "Yes, I would like that," Karoline told Ingrid. Ingrid's family welcomed the young girl with open arms to their wonderful home in the country where they had horses and much land, and she became a part of a real, loving family for six months. She did her share of household chores and enjoyed being with them.

One day she received a letter from Gustov. He asked if she would come back to Lohne and he would see if he could find her a job and said he would come to see her from Bremen, where he worked, as often as he could. *Hasn't Gustov always helped me?* she asked herself. I must do this for him.

Gustov saw an advertisement in the paper from an English officer at the nearby base who wanted a German girl to do housework and be a companion to his oriental wife in their apartment in Lohne. Gustov called him and asked him if he would interview Karoline for this job.

Though she was terribly nervous and couldn't speak a word of English, nor he German, somehow she was hired! She was to be responsible for the apartment and get it ready for his wife who would arrive in a few days. Capt. O.R. Goodrich told his little maid, through their landlady as interpreter, that he would stay at the base until Sun Lin arrived, but that Karoline's duties would be getting the food and the apartment ready. He would bring food from the base. His landlady, Helga Ritter, continued to translate his wishes between the two of them and told Karoline in German, "You will be expected to serve Capt. and Mrs. Goodrich tea and biscuits in bed each morning before he leaves for the base, and wear a dark frock with a short white apron." She made the German girl understand, and Karoline answered that she would be happy to do that.

For several days Karoline stayed in the apartment in her very own bedroom, and acquainted herself with the kitchen and its contents. She couldn't believe her good fortune and went about her duties smiling...something she had almost forgotten how to do. Her thoughts were always entwined with Gustov. She wondered what he was doing and hoped he still wanted to be with her and not one of the many other girls available to so few German men now. He worked as a tailor in his well-dressed papa's store in Bremen, and she knew how good Gustov looked in his clothes.

The day Sun Lin arrived was one of greatest apprehension for Karoline, but she needn't have had a concern. They both seemed to share similar inner feelings, and through Helga and Mrs. Gordon Wilbur Nash, on the floor above them, Capt. Goodrich felt the two could safely be left to themselves when he was at the base and teach each other their languages. They had to learn to communicate!

Days of hilarity with the three learning each others languages followed, and when Sun Lin entertained for her husband, Karoline did all the cooking, and she learned English words for each item she used…a willing learner. Mrs. Nash enjoyed it all and showed the two how to make the English dishes Capt. Goodrich would like. The two girls kept each other company when the captain was at the base and walked to the store together to buy the items needed for their planned menus.

Karoline had been working for the capt. and Sun Lin for several months, and they had become very good friends. Their communication with each other had been exceptional. It was a pretty day in May when Karoline received a much anticipated letter from Gustov. He was coming! She was so excited she couldn't think straight. When she heard the knock at the back door, she tripped over the broom, righted herself and flew to the back door of the Goodrich's apartment. It was then when she opened the door to let him in that she knew he was the only man for her. He grabbed her and kissed her so hard her knees almost buckled. "I have a job on the island of Juist in the Baltic Sea for the summer, and I want you to get a job there and go with me!" he blurted out in the only way Gustov knew. She was putty in his hands. "I will have to talk to the Goodrich's, Gustov. They have depended on me," she said, with hope lingering in her voice. "All right *we* will do that," Gustov said firmly.

The Goodriches hated to let Karoline go but knew she and Gustov should be together, so they gave her a wonderful goodbye party and bid them much good luck. "Please name your first child after us!" they said, laughing at the happy German couple. Karoline had been able to get a maid's job at the little resort's lodge on Juist Island where many tourists came each summer and was terribly excited at going for the months ahead.

The first ferry ride Karoline had ever taken was out in the Baltic Sea to Juist and was definitely something she wouldn't have chosen to do, but she thrilled at the thought of her new job and working close to

Gustov. She would have her own small room and would make beds, clean and make salads in the kitchen while Gustov did tailoring work for his employer. "It will be an easy job, Gustov, and I will have food and a bed and no worries, for the first time in my life!" she exclaimed. "Isn't that right, Gustov?" He knew his Karoline had returned to good health and answered her with a loving smile and a wink. They both liked the young couple who ran the lodge.

Gustov's tailoring job allowed them free time to see each other every night, and they strolled the beach, listening to the slapping of the cold North Sea waters along the shore. When a ferry's short blast announced their arrival, Karoline and Gustov watched the visitors file off and the docks rise and fall gently. Small rental boats bobbed back and forth tugging at their moorings, and the lapping waters rushed up the grey sand shores forming little rivulets which trickled back to the sea.

Karoline had never been this happy. She put her past behind her. Gustov said, "We are engaged. All right?" She was ecstatic, but she hoped it wouldn't be too long before they married, even if there *were* no places to live.

When the scheduled, working part of their summer ended, in his matter-of-fact-way Gustov stated, "We should stay for two more weeks before going back to Lohne." Though he did not put a question to her, she always agreed. She had become accustomed to his making all their decisions. How could she mind?

On each warm summer night, they enjoyed lying under a full moon which splashed silvery streaks across lethargic swells of the sea. She had never seen such a big moon and so many stars. It was her first vacation and one she would remember for the rest of her life!

About the end of their first vacation week, Karoline awoke one morning feeling dizzy. *Oh, she couldn't be sick again*, she thought, with a heavy heart. She had no desire to go back to Denmark and the Hartz Mts. Later that night she said, "Gustov, I don't feel good. I almost fainted this morning, but I grabbed hold of the poster bed so I wouldn't fall. Then I stopped feeling funny."

"Oh, you will be fine!" he said as he dangled his bare feet in the cool waters below the dock and watched a small boat coming toward them with its running lights on. Karoline wasn't sure he'd even *heard* her. *Had he just dismissed the whole thing?* she wondered.

The next morning was different. She was nauseated. *Only then* did it occur to her that her monthly time was late! "Oh, my God," she breathed aloud as she tried to dress. She was shaking. Later that evening they walked along the shoreline. She used all her strength to ask Gustov the question. As she dug her toes into the warm sands, she asked, "Gustov, what if I'm pregnant??"

"No, you must *not* be. We aren't married and there's no place to live," he answered as he looked into her teary eyes. There was silence for awhile. "We wait and see," he added with an unusually somber face. They said nothing more for the rest of their walk.

A couple days later they left for Lohne and their real world. Gustov continued living with his parents, and she was visiting her sister, the young girl who had now grown into a lovely young lady! Though Ereka said, "Karoline, I hope you will stay," Karoline had strong feelings that her sister was not happy living in that small apartment either. "I have been a secretary here long enough, and Pastor Stachbart has helped me so much, and he and his wife have had me to dinner most every Sunday. They have listened to all my problems. But I read an ad in the newspaper that said they were looking for one more girl to help at the Youth Hostel in Amsterdam, and Pastor said he thought it would be good for me. People go to that retreat to rest, play games or just vacation. I would have a place to sleep and my food, too, " she added as she looked anxiously into her sister's eyes for approval. Karoline watched her now grownup, slightly built little sister who had turned eighteen. Ereka's dark eyes seemed almost too large for her small, pretty face, which was framed with long, brown, shiny hair. She reminded Karoline so much of her papa. There was a long pause before the older girl answered. "Ereka, I feel you must try this job because you are ready to be out on your own, but will you please remember that we mustn't lose contact...that you will write me every week, or I will worry about you?" Needless to say, that was just what Ereka wanted to hear, and even today, 2003 the young sisters who went through so much together remain close, but far apart. Ereka married a wonderful Dutchman who had been a prisoner of the Germans in Holland and who had been caught for his work for the underground. But all her life she has remained friends with her wonderful old Pastor Stachbart who married her and her husband.

It was true. Karoline was pregnant...over a month now, and she could hardly wait for the weekends and Gustov's visits. He had *not* mentioned marriage! They met and fell into each other's arms. "Gustov, I want you to know that I am worried because I've missed two monthlies!" she said as she looked into his eyes. He said nothing. Karoline felt doomed. This is not the way she wanted her life to be.

On the following weekend she visited him at his parent's home. "Gustov, what am I going to do?" The tears started to flow.

He answered, "I have told my mother and father we are going to live with them, and we are going to get married in the Lutheran Church. They will help us. Is that good?"

Karoline's relief of her plight was overwhelming! "Well, I guess we did it all backwards," she said very solemnly to Ereka, as she fumbled with the lace on her wedding dress. "We had our honeymoon before we had our wedding!"

It was crowded when they moved in with Gustov's parents and Marianna, his surviving sister, but Gustov's father, Rudolph, was fond of his pretty, new daughter-in-law and she of him, so they all got along. She always did her share to help and anxiously awaited the birth of her baby, even though it would be too soon!

Gertrude, Rudolph and Gustov were all at work the morning when Karoline began to feel labor pains. She didn't know what to do. There was no telephone; they had no car; and she would have to take a train to the hospital. Marianna grabbed her sister-in-law and said excitedly, "We must run, Karoline, to the train that is due, or we'll have to wait too long for the next one that would get us to the hospital!" As they ran the several blocks, Karoline laced her fingers around her jostling extremities so they wouldn't bounce as much. When they reached the station, her relief was more than evident as they found the train still sitting there, rumbling in low tones as the smoke curled above it. She sat down on the bench and felt a sudden gush. Her water slid down her legs, into her shoes and a small area on the platform around her.

The whistle blew and pierced the crisp air as they clamored carefully aboard the train. "I will have to start praying again," she whispered to Marianna as the girl helped her aboard the strassenbalm. "My clothes are all wet!" she exclaimed.

As they hurried into the hospital, the lady in charge put Karoline up on a table and said, as she observed her dilation, "There is NO time to prepare you," and there she turned toward the doctors. They were across the room attending to another patient whose baby wouldn't wait. A small, wet head was slowly making its way into the world as Karoline lay on the birthing table! She was frantic. Perspiration was rolling down from her forehead as she tried to get the attention of those men in white, whom she thought were much too calm. Completely out of character, Karoline yelled, "Help! Help me!" They rushed to her side and caught little redheaded Arno before he landed on the floor.

The Karls were so happy to make room for their first grandchild that they decided to move their store to Hamburg so that their son and his wife would have their *first home* to themselves!

Karoline couldn't believe their good fortune. There were millions of German refugees, displaced persons, since 1945 and 1946 who had been on the move…move to anywhere. Anyplace to find a home to live in their own country.

Many had perished during those terrible trips in the vichwaggons, from cold, hunger, malnutrition or stress of not knowing where they would go. Karoline could never forget their trips west, their short time living back in Breslau and the little flour the Polish had given them to make into bread. They had only given the refugees a fish and some flour when they sent them off in the railcars. Even while she nursed her little Arno, she shuddered to think of what her past had done to her. Surely her new life with Gustov would be wonderful, and nothing more could happen to hurt them as Hitler's war years had done to them, the Jews and their country. She shivered.

Months went by, and Karoline was so happy she felt forebodings on what could possibly come about. One night when Gustov came home from work he said,"Karoline, we don't want to stay in Germany.

What can we do here!?" he asked his young wife who was now expecting again.

"Oh, Gustov, not leave Germany!! Where would we go?" It was 1954.

"I have contacted the authorities at the Emigration Office, and they say we must come down there," he said with his eyes fairly dancing! It shocked her. She knew her husband had asperations on getting ahead, but he really hadn't said enough to her that she had any idea on how serious he was on starting a new life...away! But then she should have known. It was his German way!

As the days went by, Karoline could tell how happy and really excited Gustov was about their hopes for a new adventure. They went down to the Emigration Office to find out when they could leave and those in command said, "You cannot go until your wife has had her baby! That is the law!" They couldn't believe what they were hearing. Gustov showed his unhappiness, and Karoline felt like it was all her fault that she was holding her husband back from his great wish to leave Germany. She knew they wouldn't be able to leave until the baby was old enough to travel, so this terrible feeling of despair would be with her for months. How could they be happy?

Chapter 9: An Ocean Away

It was now 1958. Karoline had had their little girl, whom she named Ingrid after her favorite nurse. She passed her health regulations and made her Gustov the happiest tailor around. "Now we can go to America, Karoline, and make for ourselves a new and better life!" he said as he grabbed and squeezed her. They had had to get many papers together which were required for their passage aboard the General Langfit; and to ensure authorities they had a place to live, people to sponsor them in America, their good health and most important, the promised job for Gustov.

But Gertrude and Rudolph were not happy. They didn't tell little Arno much except that he would get to go on a BIG boat. "You will go out on the ocean, Arno, an ocean away from Germany!" They couldn't bring themselves to be happy over saying goodbye to their first grandchild, and they so wanted Gustov to help them with their new clothing store in Hamburg.

"You will have a long ride on the big boat, Arno, and you will see the big statue in America's harbor when we get there...the Statue of Liberty! Just wait; you will see!" promised Gustov. Karoline was full of apprehension. She was most fearful of their future but didn't dare complain to Gustov. He must not know how worried she was about their new life, so she never cried where he could see her. How happy I have made him because he thinks I'm in complete agreement with him on this new venture.

Karoline had continued to remain hopeful that this move would not come about. She thought about Ereka and her husband, Andre Bogaarden, who was so active in the resistence movement since the German police had surrounded Jewish quarters in Amsterdam. 400

young men were sent to concentration camps—extermination camps by the men in black—the SS, the elite Schutzataffel, who were wearing the death's head cap emblem. From that time on, Andre was a part of the resistence. Jews were beaten by the Dutch Nazis, and riots followed. Fabrikation, the round up of Jews, stopped March 3, 1943. For any remaining there, it was too late to leave. In Paris at the Reich's embassy, a seventeen-year-old Polish Jew shot and killed one of the secretaries of the Reich in revenge for the Nazi's treatment of Jews. Retaliation by the Nazis was a bitter vengeance. A night of murderous attacks on Jews, their businesses, shops and synagogues was from then on known as Kristallnacht, for the great amount of broken glass that littered German streets. Thirty-five Jews were killed and thousands arrested. After insurance was paid to those who were attacked, their money was confiscated by the government.

The Dutch underground watched German soldiers enter their Jewish neighbors' homes and drag the crying inhabitants out, and that was what sent underground forces of Amsterdam into a frenzied swing of action. They were all well aware of their fate if they were caught in crimes against the Reich. They were in constant danger, but under amazing secrecy they transported Jews not allowed to travel and helped many to get out of the country and hid thousands more. The Dutch Underground transported people in carts, mourner's carriages and ferried many to neutral Sweden.

Karoline learned of the fate of her childhood friends, the Howitts, Harriett, Abe, and young Harriett and Joel who had lived in Breslau. The Neidenfranks had brought the family into their home and through a passageway from their kitchen which led down a hidden stairway to a cellar filled with coal. Back of it was a small, invisible room where they hid the Howitts. Their hosts sneaked food to them and did what they could to make them comfortable.

Karoline wondered when she would ever see Ereka and Andre again. She would just have to wait. It was a beautiful, late spring day when Gustov came bounding through the door and grabbed her! "We leave next week," he said, with his voice raised to a pitch she'd never even heard!

That week went by so fast she wasn't even sure what items she had gathered together that were most needed for them to transport so far. She couldn't forget their cherished and long waited for Rosenthal dishes. There was the little, white baby bed, the blue-trimmed, white potty, their silverware and the most important possession of all, Gustov's sewing machine, his equipment for his new job in America. Their clothes went into scratched and worn suitcases.

Puffy, white clouds skittered across the azure, blue sky on July 12, 1958, their last day in Germany. It's one thing to move, thought Karoline, but to leave your homeland, what family you have left, to travel an ocean away to a land and language you scarcely knew?? She was frightened. She hadn't been this frightened during the bombings, because when they came out of the shelters, they were still in their homeland. When he wasn't looking at her—which was most often the case, anyway—she wiped away the flood of tears. But hadn't Gustov always helped her through terrible tragedies...and hadn't he always been right?

The distraught, twenty-seven-year-old mother tried to hide the salty tears as they tickled and streamed down her firm cheeks and into the corners of her quivering, full lips. She wiped them away with the back of her hand. Gustov must not see. She needn't have worried! Exuberant, red-headed Gustov Karl at that moment seemed to have forgotten her existence. He was singing, waving his arms and dancing in circles to the oompah-pahs of the pounding, colorfully dressed bon voyage band!

Karoline brushed aside her dark, windblown curls as the tears continued to plague her vision. As she stood on the sun-faded, long, wooden dock next to her husband, she held fifteen-month old, squirming Ingrid; and tugging at her light, summer skirt, as she tried desperately to keep up with Gustov, was Arno. She was sure he knew, even at three years of age, the finality of this goodbye. His Oma Karl's tearful hugs had not been like any other.

"Come, Karoline, don't be so slow...keep up with me!" he shouted above the sounds of crying children, loud chatter and nervous laughter. The summer air in the Port of Bremerhaven was saturated with so many languages. It was a chance of a lifetime, Gustov had told her...a better life in a new land!

Follow. Keep up! Karoline. That was the German way she thought to herself. Yells of goodbye, laughing, crying and waving rent the air.

She shuddered as she tried to vision such a large body of water. The only boat she'd ever been on was the little ferry she and Gustov had taken to Juist that summer, the summer when the war was over, that *romantic* summer she would never forget!

Suddenly, the band launched into a familiar, sad tune, Nun Adeau! "So Goodbye, My Homeland..." and little Ingrid's attention was drawn to the jumping, brightly dressed (in German lederhosens,) portly musicians! Ingrid's tiny fingers had found the cord around her mother's neck which was attached to the ID number, a requirement of the organization which formed this emigration movement.

As they walked along the weathered, shifting docks, Karoline looked high above. She couldn't *believe* the size of this ship! In spite of the warm, summer day, she shivered. I have nothing to compare this experience to, but I *must* survive it was uppermost in her mind.

Hundreds of emigrants from all over Europe—Germans, Russians and Polish—were among them, and had shoved and pushed their way toward the rope-framed gangplank which led to the decks of the mammoth General Langfit, a former troop carrying ship! She supposed to Gustov it looked like a castle, but to her it meant ten days of rocking imprisonment.

Arno looked up, up and UP and tripped as he tried to see the ship's topmost mast!

"Arno, pass auf!" she warned, as she got as firm a grip on his warm, sweaty little hand as she could. He really didn't need more to cry over. Gustov wouldn't like that.

Blue skies stretched above, and the brilliance of the sun's rays striking the freshly-painted vessel nearly blinded them as they strained to behold the size of their transport moored at this port near the North Sea.

Walking slowly up the steep, long gangplank, Karoline's clumsy, black shoes found leverage in the wooden grooves, but she was barely able to keep her balance. Then the shrill scream of the bosan's whistle rent the summer air and made shivers run up her spine.

"Mutti, what is that?" cried Arno fearfully, as he grabbed his mother's hand with both of his own.

Karoline tried to contribute a nonchalance in her answer when she said, "That is a beautiful whistle you must learn to enjoy, Arno!"

They reached the railing high above the docks and looked frantically below for Gustov's parents and sister. "There they are!" yelled Gustov above the raucous chattering of the emigrants. Gertrude and Rudolph caught sight of their little family and waved and threw kisses, but Karoline knew only too well how unhappy they were, as her own unhappiness more than matched theirs.

A mighty, low, thundering blast from the General Langfit ripped the warm air, and the clanging sounds from the weighing of anchor reached their ears. Seagulls squawked angrily as they flew wildly from serene perches aboard the ship to find solace elsewhere.

They were ready for departure. Karoline trembled. Suddenly, yet silently, the massive hull moved slowly away from the pier causing scarcely a ripple in the dark, green, cold, deep waters of the harbor.

"Now we go to the North Sea, Karoline!" shouted Gustov, looking at her with dancing, green eyes. "Look, Arno," he yelled as he held the child high, "we go now to the English Channel, then on to America, an ocean away, and see the Statue of Liberty!"

References

These I Do Remember by Gerde Hass
World Atlas
Breslau Rand McNally Atlas of World History
Kish, George's World Geography
The Inextinguishable Symphony by Martin Goldsmith
What Did You Do in the War, Daddy? Sabine Riechel
Stones from the River by Ursula Hegi
Rand McNally Kish, Geo.'s World
Germany, Marshall Dill, Jr.
Mothers in the Fatherland by Koontz
Time Table of History by Bernard Gruen
Customs by Times Books
Atlas of World History
Time Life Books
Call Us To Witness by Warfield, Hanis
A Man in the Middle by Sagejlle, Witold 1910
Germany, West Germany & Berlin by Michelan
Mutter & Volk, Protestant Magazine
Germany – History of the Nazi Party 1918 – 33 943.0085
Germany – Description & Travel 940.542
German Language R433 Betteridge
Germany – History 940.542
Germany, History of the Nazi Party 943.085 1918-1933
Germany, Description and Travel 914.3An
Mutter Kreug
Hitler in Color
The Convoys in the Cold Atlantic

Poland 1939-1947 by John Contonvidis
The Promise Hitler Kept by Adolph Folkmann
The Rape of Poland by Mikolajazyk, Stanislaw
McMillan World Gazeteer & Geographical Direction
The Columbia Lippencott Gazeteer of the World, Columbia University Press1952
Ambassador World Atlas
Germany, Marshall Dill, Jr.

Printed in the United States
22506LVS00002B/92

9 781413 706567